Just *When You* Thought

Just *When You* Thought

A Novel

by Patricia E. Turner

5th Street Books
Snellville, Georgia

Published by: 5th Street Books
P O Box 391633
Snellville, Georgia 30039
www.5thstreetbooks.com

First Edition 2006

Library of Congress Control Number: 2006900862

ISBN 10 digit: 0-9776359-4-5
ISBN 13 digit: 978-0-9776359-4-8

5th Street Books is a Trademark of Alpha Omega Entertainment, LLC.

Manufactured in the United States of America

*This book is dedicated to
my granddaughter Zoree, whom
I have not seen since her birth.*

ACKNOWLEDGMENTS

God, my faith in you is abundant. You have proven to me over and over again that all things are possible through you. Truly, deeply faith is the substance of things hoped for and the evidence of things not seen.

My husband Kent, thank you for being my strength, my rock and inspiration. I could not have done this without you.

My son Demarlo, thank you for being a visionary. Your life has changed my life.

My son Carlo, thank you for coming back home to me from the war in Iraq. I am so proud of you.

A special thank you to Lori Carangelo, for allowing excerpts from her website listed in the back of this book.

A baby is God's opinion that life should go on.

—CARL SANDBURG (1878–1967)

Chapter 1

The year was 1976, in the heart of the south, a small urban city in Georgia that most people would call a ghetto. A baby girl named Mekia was born to a fourteen-year-old girl named Katie. She did not know who the father of her baby girl was, so we'll leave it at that. My name is Mekia James and this is my story. Now, this is not just any old story. This story will make you think twice before trusting anyone. After you read my story, you will never listen to the words, "I love you," again.

I was the oldest of three children and the only child

my mother had who did not know who her father was. My other siblings grew up sharing memories with their daddies, but that was okay, because I was sort of a loner. I took the role of leader in the house to help my mom. That gave me something worthwhile to do.

My mother, Katie, was my life; she was beautiful, kind and loving. Katie had long, black hair, fair skin and a great figure. I wanted to believe she was perfect, but Katie had a problem—men. Katie would go through men like it meant nothing to her. I watched her for years going in and out of relationships and I used to think to myself, *I am not going to be like Katie; I will find the perfect man to marry.* Katie couldn't pick the right man if her life depended on it. She was on her fifth man in six months and that relationship was coming to an end.

Watching Katie made me think about my life, and I was desperate to keep from becoming like her. Her poor judgments made life hard for my brother, my sister and me. But in spite of all the things she did and did not do, I still loved her.

My grandmother died of cancer at a young age. She had only one other sister, Aunt Maggie, and she was the only other family we had. Katie would never let us visit her though, and she would never say why. I remember Aunt Maggie because she always sent me something in the mail for my birthday and if I needed anything, I could call her. I tried to ask Katie to visit Aunt Maggie more, but Katie got upset when I asked her about it. Sometimes I would sneak over to visit Aunt Maggie when I had money to ride the bus to her house. Aunt Maggie lived in a small subdivision of Clayton County. Her house was brick with two bedrooms and two bathrooms.

The neighborhood was quiet, and it seemed like a great place to live. Aunt Maggie had never married; she had no children and lived alone.

We lived on Fairburn Street in what we called the *good part* of the ghetto. I guess it was called that because the hard-core hoodlums didn't hang around our building. Our building was on top of a hill with one other building unit. There were no trees, no bushes, just brick buildings. This made it hard for the hoodlums to hide and sell drugs like they wanted to.

Peewee, my cousin, and his mother, Anna, lived in the same building as we did, and Ms. Anna was good at calling the police on anybody. Anna liked to plant flowers and she did not want to see her flowers ruined, so she would call the police on anyone who walked by if she didn't know them. This made the dealers stay away from the top of the hill, the good part of the ghetto. Folks said Ms. Anna was a little bit touched, but I don't know. I thought she was a nice lady.

By the way, Peewee was not my real cousin; we just pretended to be cousins. Peewee was a big dude about three hundred pounds, and everyone in the hood knew him and knew not to cross him. I never knew why. I made friends with him to keep boys away from me that I didn't want to be bothered with. Somehow it worked. I didn't want to be caught up in any relationship with the boys in the hood. I knew it would be a dead end for me. Watching Katie destroy herself, there was no way I could do that to myself. There wasn't a whole lot for me to do, so I spent a lot of time at Peewee's house watching him play videos. Being with Peewee was a good front for me.

Chapter 2

One day, Katie met a man named Johnny. He was tall with brown skin, well built, and had low cut hair. He always dressed well and had small eyes that could pierce through your skin. Johnny never said much to me, but I didn't trust him. Katie, on the other hand, loved him. I think Katie really fell for this one. She started allowing him to spend the night until finally, he moved some of his things into the house. Even though it was only a few things, you could tell he was the kind of guy who had his own place. I don't think

Katie ever thought for a second he had another place. Johnny became so comfortable staying at our house that he would walk around nude.

Katie wouldn't say a word to him. I really hated him for doing this, and I started to disrespect Katie for allowing it. I thought about my baby sister; she was only eight, and she should not have to see that damned Johnny walking through our apartment nude. It was bad enough I had to see him that way. I hated Johnny more than words could describe, but most of all, I feared him. He was the kind of man that forced fear into your body just by being in the same room. Katie always had some man living with us, but this time, it was different. When Johnny was in the house, I couldn't sleep. I thought about a movie I had seen where the father raped the daughter over and over again, and I thought about Johnny doing the same thing to me one day, or worse, to my sister. I kept having the same dream about Johnny coming into my room and doing something really bad to me. I wanted to tell Aunt Maggie about it, but I was afraid.

Months went by and Katie seemed to be getting along great with Johnny. The good thing about their relationship was they stayed in Katie's room most of the time. Johnny started wandered around the house late at night when Katie was asleep or when she was drugged out. Every night I could hear him creeping around. Sometimes I would open my door and peep out at him. Something inside made me think he knew that I was watching and he loved every moment of it. I thought really hard about killing him, but I knew I wouldn't be able to get away with such a thing. I never knew Johnny's last name; he was just Johnny to me. My mother loved that fool even though he would lie, cheat and steal from her. She put up with his shit for a long time, until one day they got into a really bad fight. It was late at night, after 2:00 a.m., and I could hear them yelling in Katie's bedroom.

I heard Katie ask Johnny, "Why did you take my stuff?"

Then I heard Johnny tell Katie she was out of control. He told her if she didn't pull herself together, he would leave her. The fight continued for what seemed like hours. Katie accused Johnny of having other women.

I heard him say to her, "What do you expect me to do, stay here with your drunken, drugged out ass?" He continued, "Why should I do that when I could have any woman out there?"

This made Katie furious; she threw a lamp at Johnny. When I heard the lamp break, I got up to see if Katie was okay. When I got to Katie's bedroom door, Johnny was leaving and Katie was shouting, "Get out and don't ever come back, you bastard!"

Johnny looked at me, smiled and winked his eye, then looked at Katie and said, "You will regret this day," and he left the house. All I could do was to thank God he was gone. Finally, I was able to sleep again.

Six months passed and I was happy to have my mother back. No more Johnny, no more late night walks, and no more sleepless nights. Katie was finally back to being herself. She started cooking for the family again and making sure the house was clean. She cooked Sunday dinner and took us to the movies. We were a family again. I was so happy.

One morning when I got up, I looked in the mirror and noticed I was developing. My breasts were getting large and my butt was beginning to form. I looked at my hair and noticed how long and hard to manage it had gotten. I forgot about everything else and asked Katie if she would braid my hair for me. She agreed and started braiding my hair every week. She even braided my baby sister's hair.

Being excited about Katie, I went to see Peewee to tell him how great Katie was doing. He said the word in the hood was Johnny had Katie doing drugs, but I didn't care what people said. It was just nice to have Katie back to her old self again.

Chapter 3

Winter finally passed and spring was in full bloom. One day, while Katie was braiding my hair, someone knocked on the front door. Katie went to see who it was. I stood behind her as she looked through the peephole. Katie stood there for a minute like she didn't want to open the door. I asked, "What's wrong, Katie?"

"Nothing girl, just be quiet," she replied softly. Then she opened the door and I saw Johnny standing there with a bag of groceries and a stupid look on his face. I knew he was up to no good, and I thought if Katie let him come back, my world would end. Katie looked back at me and saw the disturbed look on my face, then she pushed me and told me to go to my room. I ran to my room crying and stayed there listening to Johnny tell Katie lies about how he missed her. I peeped through my bedroom door and saw Johnny kissing Katie. She looked like she loved every moment of it. I knew then, Johnny was back for good.

I looked in the mirror and promised myself there was no way I would do that to a daughter of mine. Then I noticed the few braids Katie had completed in my hair, and I knew she wouldn't be braiding my hair anymore. Sadly, I took the braids out. My other two siblings were not at home; they were with their daddies, so I had no one to talk to. I stared in the mirror at my hair, and then I put it in a ponytail. As I looked in the mirror, I began to get sad thinking about Johnny being back in our house, so I went to Peewee's to talk with him.

Peewee suggested I just pretend like Johnny was not there, and eventually Katie would see what type of fool he was and get rid of him. Peewee may have been a big guy, but he wasn't the best person to get advice from, so I didn't really think about what he told me. I just sat there watching him play videos. Soon it began to get dark, so I told Peewee I had to go and headed home. When I got there, Katie's bedroom door was closed. Johnny was still there, which meant he would be spending the night. My stomach began to turn inside out with sickness. I knew I would not get any sleep that night. How could Katie do this to me?

It was around 3:30 a.m. when I heard the floorboards

creak. It was Johnny coming down the hall that led to my room. He had made that trip several times before, but something had always stopped him from coming into my room.

This time it was different; he continued down the hall until he reached my bedroom door. Johnny came in and closed the door quietly behind him. It was then that I saw him tiptoeing toward my bed. As I peeped up at him, I could see his naked body and the part of him I never wanted to see exposed. I lay there on my back with the covers pulled up to my neck. I was terrified, pretending to be asleep.

The bed shifted as he crawled onto it. He then moved on top of me and I could feel his nude body as he moved slowly, but firmly. Then he did the unthinkable. He started to put his penis inside of me. I was terrified, but I could not scream. I managed to slowly reach under my pillow and pull out a knife I had hidden just for this moment. I cut Johnny down the middle of his face as hard as I could. He jumped up yelling and ran out of my room. There was blood all over my bed. I heard Katie ask him what happened, but I did not stay to hear what his answer was.

I ran out of the house and hid in the backyard. I could see the street from where I hid, and I watched Johnny run out to his car with a towel on his face and drive away. I was so scared that Katie would not believe me or be mad at me for what I had done, so I stayed in the backyard for a while until I began to get scared of the night sounds.

Eventually I made it back into the house and when I got to my room, Katie was sitting on my bed crying. She looked up at me and said, "I know what happened. That dirty bastard raped you, didn't he?"

With tears rolling down my face, I said, "No, but he tried to."

Katie held me and said, "You don't have to worry about Johnny anymore. He is gone for good." I was so relieved knowing Katie was not mad at me. I realized my mother loved me more than I thought she did. Katie admitted to me that she had been using drugs with Johnny and promised never to do it again. I really wanted to believe Katie, but I couldn't. I knew she would still be the same old Katie, someone I never wanted to be.

Chapter 4

Things finally got back to normal in our house when Johnny was gone. Months had passed since he left, and Katie never said a word about him. She said she had a new man friend, but she never brought him to the house and that was fine with me. I was happy Johnny was gone, but deep down Katie seemed sad. I thought she might still be trying to get Johnny out of her system, but I hoped she would be back to her old self soon.

It was the day before my fourteenth birthday. *Oh*

boy! I said to myself. Oh boy, indeed. Katie sent me to the store for groceries. While I was there, I saw a boy who caught my eye. He was so cute, almost too cute. I said to myself, *He would never notice someone like me,* so I pretended not to notice him. I guess he hadn't seen me or pretended not to see me, because our eyes never met, and I left the store and didn't think of him again that day. After all, my birthday was coming and I had no time to waste on a boy.

The next day was my birthday and Peewee was throwing me a birthday party at his house. It was supposed to have been a surprise, but I found out anyway. I arrived at the party early, at about 8:00 p.m. I wasn't much of a party person and Peewee knew it, which led me to wonder if Peewee was throwing the party for another reason. You could never tell with Peewee; he always did things spontaneously. But since he said he was throwing the party for me, I had to attend. The house was packed. The want-to-be hoodlums even showed up. I could not believe Anna had let this many people past her flowers. I finally found Peewee and asked, "How did you convince Anna to agree to inviting this many people?"

Peewee replied, with a big smile on is face, "Anna is out of town and she won't be back for a week!"

I said to myself, *Oh, shit, this is going to be a long night.*

Peewee had somehow gotten a DJ to come and spin the music. This DJ was so good he even had me nodding my head to the beat. I strolled through the party trying to find someone to have a decent conversation with. My eyes landed on a boy standing in the corner with a drink in his hand, nodding his head to the music. It was Mr. Too Cute, the guy I had seen in the grocery store the day before. I quickly turned my head and started back toward Peewee to give him the 411, but I couldn't find him anywhere.

When I turned around, I saw Mr. Too Cute coming my way. There was nowhere for me to go, so I stood there trying to be cool, nodding my head and sipping on some ginger ale. He came up to me and introduced himself as Don Robinson, and then he asked me to dance. I hesitated, trying to be cool, but knowing all along I wanted to dance with him.

"Let me finish my drink," I said.

He replied, "You can take your drink with you on the dance floor."

I looked at him. "Okay," I agreed with a smile, but I put the drink down anyway before heading to the dance floor. Just as we started to dance, the DJ switched on The Ojays singing, *Let Me Make Love to You, Baby. I knew this damned DJ was going to get me in trouble.* Don and I danced, looking into each other's eyes. Then Don asked me what my name was.

"It's Mekia," I said.

He replied, "Mekia...that's a beautiful name for a beautiful woman. You must be the birthday girl."

"Yes, I am. How did you guess that?"

"Peewee told everyone he was throwing a birthday party for the cutest girl in the hood," he said.

"He did? That Peewee is something else," I said with a smile.

"Yeah, he is," Don agreed. We dance and talked, and before the night was over, Don had mesmerized me. I knew he would be the man I would marry someday. I had found Mr. Right.

It was almost eleven and I knew I had to get home before 11:30, or Katie would kill me. I never could understand why Katie always wanted me to be home before 11:30; she was never at home when I got there, but I still tried to be a good girl. I hoped that would keep me from being like Katie. In the back of my mind, I wondered how long I could be this good girl while I dated Don. Then I thought to myself, *Who cares? I am going to marry him anyway.*

Don walked me home and I tried to make the walk last as long as I could. We finally reached my apartment. I wanted to talk longer, but I didn't want Don to know how excited I was about him. We exchanged phone numbers and I had my first kiss; it was perfect! The next day I told Katie about Don. She was not thrilled about me dating, especially someone four years older than me. I believed she was worried about me because she'd had such bad luck with men. But she did not have to worry, because Don was nothing like the men she dated. I was so excited about Don, and went on and on about him to Katie. Katie did not say a lot to me about him, she just said, "You be careful, now."

"What do you mean?" I asked.

"Just be careful, Mekia," Katie repeated.

I thought to myself, *Be careful? Is that all she can say? Can't she see I am in love? I have found the perfect man.*

Don and I had been dating for months by this point. We talked on the phone and he took me to the movies. Don did not have a car so we rode the bus everywhere we went. I really enjoyed spending time with Don, but there was something about him I just couldn't figure out. Don was tall, with brown skin, curly hair and a great body. He was the kind of guy the girls would call 'eye candy.' I figured he was mixed with something, but who knew? Everyone was mixed with something, even me. Katie said her grandmother was Indian, but I had never seen her; she died before I was born. Most people say I am pretty, but I never saw myself that way. If you asked Peewee to described me, he would say I am bright skinned, with light brown eyes, long, black wavy hair, nice legs, with a great figure—the cutest girl in the hood. Don seemed to love the way I looked; he could not take his eyes off me when we were together.

Now, the question of sex had not come up between us yet and I was kind of glad, because I was still a virgin and not ready for sex. One night, Don called me on the phone. I was happy to hear from him and I knew he would ask to come over. I was always excited for him to come over. Katie was not at home; she had gone out with a friend. Don came over around nine and we were in my room talking when suddenly the sex question came up. Not with words, but with Don putting his hands in my pants and sucking on my breast. I had really large breasts and Don was really enjoying himself, and so was I. Then all of a sudden, something came over me and I got scared.

"Don, stop," I said.

"Why? What's wrong?" he asked.

"I can't do this," I replied. I was really thinking about Johnny trying to rape me and how I had to cut his face.

Don got upset and said, "Okay, I guess I better be going." I wanted to tell him to stay, but I would've had to tell him about Johnny, and I never wanted to talk about that to anyone. I thought I had gotten over that night, but somehow it still haunted me every now and then. Katie never talked to me about it and I wondered why.

Two weeks had passed. Don had not called and I hadn't seen him hanging out in any of the usual places in the hood. Don did not live in the hood, he just hung out there, and I never knew why. I wondered if he would ever call me again, and what I would say to him if he did. I told Katie that Don and I'd had a fight, but she never asked any questions or gave me any advice. Hell, she never even looked at me. This really bugged me. It hurt. And I always wondered why she put on a false show of pretending not to care. I never said anything else to Katie about Don and she never asked.

I went to school every day, came home and stayed in my room, secretly hoping Don would call me. After six weeks had passed, I began to forget about Mr. Too Cute Don. I decided it was time to get on with my life. I started hanging out with Peewee again, watching him play videos and shit. One day, while I was at Peewee's house, he asked me what had happened between big Johnny and Katie.

"They broke it off," I said simply.

"Why?" Peewee asked.

"I don't know," I replied.

"I heard from a couple of people that big Johnny was in some kind of accident," Peewee said.

"What do you mean he was in an accident?"

"They said he was in an accident and got his face scarred up pretty bad. Word is he left town to try to get some plastic surgery, but the doctors aren't sure it will work. They say it was so bad he almost died."

I looked at Peewee and said, "I'm sure he will be all right. He seemed to be the kinda guy who could take care of himself."

"I hope you are right," he said.

I nodded. "I hope I am right, too."

Chapter 5

GIF, I thought to myself. I had not had a good day at school; I was thinking about what Peewee had told me about Johnny. Then my mind flashed: *He deserved everything he got.* As soon as I opened the door, I saw Katie sitting on the couch looking crazy and she insisted I go to the store for milk. I'd had a tough day and I really didn't want to be bothered with Katie or go to the damned store for her. I looked in the refrigerator and saw there was milk already there and told her so. She said she needed fresh milk, and I thought to myself,

What the hell does she need fresh milk for? She never cooks anymore.

Katie had stopped cooking and cleaning the house again. She was staying out all night and we could never have a decent conversation like we used to. She was always either out with some man friend or locked in her room when she was home. She never brought this new friend home and I always wondered why. Katie went on and on about the milk in the refrigerator that was spoiled, and how she wanted to make cookies. I was so sick of her crying about the damned milk that I gave in and went to the store for her.

I arrived at the store around 4:30 p.m. It was Friday, so it was crowded. Everybody and their damned grandmother was in the store. Boy, was I mad at Katie. As I walked through the store, another thought flashed through my mind: *She must be on those damned drugs again.* I went to the dairy aisle, grabbed a gallon of milk and headed to the checkout line. As I stood in line, someone came up behind me and whispered in my ear, "You are the finest girl in this store. How are you?" I spun around to find Don. I was mad at him, but happy to see him at the same time.

Then he gave me some bullshit story about how he had been miserable without me, but he wanted to give me some time and space. I didn't respond. "Can I take you out tomorrow night?" he asked.

Before I could stop myself, the word "yes" came out of my mouth. "Damn," I muttered to myself. "That was stupid." Still, I went home happy that I had run into Don at the store.

After a dream-filled nap, I decided to see if Katie

had finished the cookies she said she was going to bake. I went into the kitchen, but there were no cookies to be found. I could hear Katie in her room with one of her men friends, and I was surprised she had finally brought someone home. I knew she would not make the damned cookies.

The next morning I got up happy, knowing I had a date with Don. Katie was still sleeping in her room and I could smell the scent of sex coming from under her door. *Who knows what kind of guy she has in there with her. What kinda mother has Katie turned into?* I wondered. After what happened with Johnny, I thought she would never let any of her friends sleep over again. Once again, I promised myself I would never be like her.

I left and went to Peewee's house to cry on his shoulder, but he was the one who really needed my shoulder to cry on. He told me his mother had a nervous breakdown and she was in the hospital. He was going to see her later.

"I'm so sorry, Peewee," I told him. "Do you want me to go with you to the hospital?"

"No thanks," he replied. "She's only allowed to have family visit."

Later, I asked Peewee if he knew a guy named Don he had invited to the party.

"No, I don't," he replied. "Someone else probably invited him. I just put the word out there about the party. You know it don't take long to get the word about a party around here."

"Well anyway, I'm dating him. We have a date tonight. What do you think, Peewee?" I asked.

He looked at me and said, "Go for it, girl."

I looked at Peewee and thought, *Hmm, that's unusual for him not to have much to say. He must be preoccupied thinking about his mother.* So, I left and went home.

Don picked me up Saturday at my house around six. He was driving a white mustang. I thought to myself, *This is a mighty fine car.* It looked new, but I didn't know anything about cars. He said his mom had given it to him for his birthday. Don was excited about the car and so was I. Don had turned eighteen years old during the time we hadn't seen each other. He looked so fine to me that I could barely take my eyes off him. Somehow I knew if I got into that car, my life would never be the same, but I got in anyway. I was blinded by love.

Don asked me where I wanted to go, something he had never asked me before.

"Wherever you want to go," I said.

"I know this great place I want to show you where we can talk and I can beg you to forgive me," he said.

"Where is this place?" I asked him.

"Dove Park," he replied. As we drove to the park, Don talked about how much he missed me and how glad he was we had run into each other at the store. As I sat silently listening to Don, I noticed there was something different about him. When we reached the park, Don parked his car in a secluded area. There were several other cars there; it was just like the drive-in movie theatre, but without the movie.

Don continued to talk until he noticed I was not really responding to him, then he stopped. He asked me what was wrong and I told him something seemed different about him. He said, "That's because I am eighteen. I'm a man now." With that, he began to kiss, touch, feel, and suck all over me, and I did not resist him. We had sex.

I was only fourteen years old. What was I thinking having sex? I did not want to end up like Katie with three children, no hope, no future, no dreams of success, no husband, and nothing to look forward to. But at the same time, I did not want to take the chance of losing Don again, so I didn't stop him this time. Afterwards, we went to get something to eat and Don took me home around eleven.

That night I lay in my bed wondering if Don would come back or if he would disappear like so many of Katie's man friends. I lay there for hours until I finally fell asleep. When I awoke, it was morning and the phone was ringing. It was Don. He told me he had a surprise for me and asked if he could come by and pick me up. I agreed. Katie still wasn't home and I wondered where she was. I walked through the house and saw no sign that Katie had been home. I started to worry about her and thought she must be doing drugs heavily. I hoped she would be all right. Then I wondered if maybe, I should call Aunt Maggie, but I didn't. I was too excited about Don coming over.

When Don arrived, he had a small box in his hands. "What's in the box?" I asked.

He gave it to me and said, "Open it."

I opened the box and saw a necklace with a diamond in it. "This means you are my lady, and there is nothing I wouldn't do for you," he said. I was so happy. All of my fears of losing Don were over. Just then, Katie walked in and saw us kissing, but she didn't say a word to us. She walked past us and went to her bedroom, slamming the door. Don and I left and went for a ride in the park.

Don and I saw each other every day. He would take me to school and pick me up. When we got to my house, we always went to my room to have sex. I wondered if Katie knew. Don and I had gotten to know each other really well, but there was still something about him I couldn't figure out. Whatever it was about him, it couldn't be that bad. He was the perfect man for me.

Chapter 6

After dating Don for a year and two months, he took me to meet his family, which was something I thought would never happen. I finally got the chance to meet his mother, Ruby, and his sister, Danielle. Don had told me that his father was dead and he didn't like to talk about it. I sensed the topic of his father was sensitive to the whole family, so I left it alone.

Ruby was a pretty lady in her early fifties. She had black, velvet hair, warm eyes, and fair skin. She looked like she was of Italian descent. Danielle could go as a white girl. She was twenty-five with long, black hair and dark, brown eyes, and a great body. She looked nothing like her mother or Don. Ruby took to me right away and I felt very comfortable around her. Danielle, on the other hand, did not say much to me; she just looked me over as if something was wrong with me. I was very uncomfortable when she was around. After I had gotten used to being around Don's family, I finally asked him what Danielle's problem was. He said, "Don't pay her any mind. She is just jealous." So I left it at that.

Don's mother's house was in Dekalb County, an area where some of the well-to-do black families lived. It was a four-bedroom, brick house with a two-car garage. The house was beautiful, especially compared to where I lived. *One day I will have a house like this, just for me and Don*, I dreamed. Life was good.

I was in my senior year of high school and I was happy! Don and I had been dating for three years by this point. Things were going great. Don had a job working where he must have been making good money, because he always bought me anything I wanted. Funny, I never knew where Don worked. I never asked and he never mentioned it. We talked about getting married, having two children and moving to northern Georgia. I was sooo happy!

Katie had been staying in her room more and more these days. When she did come out, I could barely stand to look at her. She looked bad and smelled bad too. I called Aunt Maggie, the only person I knew who would come and help. Aunt Maggie came and took Katie to the hospital. The doctor told us it was good that we got her to the hospital when we did. He said Katie was dehydrated and at the stage of an overdose of cocaine. I sat there with Aunt Maggie listening to the doctor and thinking how happy I was that I called Aunt Maggie when I did. Katie stayed in the hospital for three months. I went to see her everyday. Until, finally the doctor told her she could go home. When she came home, she was much better. She looked at me and said, "Thank you for calling Aunt Maggie." Then she went to her room and closed the door. She slept the entire day.

The next morning, Katie was up cooking breakfast and singing. I went into the kitchen and out of nowhere, she kissed me and gave me a hug. I was in shock, but happy she was better. Katie looked at me and said, "I promise this time. I really promise to stop." I didn't say anything to her; I just continued to hug her because I knew that moment would not last. Katie was supposed to attend a drug rehabilitation center for therapy, after her release from the hospital. She never did.

Graduation was six months away, and I was excited and feeling great. I could finally make Katie proud of me on graduation day. It was a busy time for me at school. I would be graduating with honors and I was in charge of the yearbook.

Four months from graduation, I got really sick and couldn't get out of bed to go to school. Katie said I probably had a 24-hour bug, and it would go away in a day or two. After two days passed, and I still didn't feel any better, Katie took me to the doctor. We waited for hours to see him until it was finally my turn, but that's what happens when you go to a county hospital. The doctor examined me and sent me back out to wait with Katie. Finally, he called us into his office and told me I was four weeks pregnant.

All I could think about was being like Katie. I should have been taking birth control. All the girls in school talked about it and we even had classes about it. Why didn't Katie talk to me about birth control? She wasn't always on drugs. Surely she knew Don and I were having sex. What in the world would I do now?

When we left the doctor's office and got into the car, the first thing Katie said was, "How could you ruin your life by getting pregnant? Didn't you learn anything from me?" She yelled at me all the way home. Once we got to the house, I was so tired of her yelling at me and telling me how my life was ruined, I started to yell back at her.

"I probably wouldn't be pregnant if you had talked to me," I cried. "You could have done something instead of thinking I was this perfect, young girl who went to school and stayed in her room reading. I wasn't reading in my room. Don and I fucked in my room for three years. How could you not know, or did you even care? You probably wanted me to be just like you! But it will never happen, because Don will marry me and take me away from seeing you come in and out of the house with a different man and having fucking sessions while you're on drugs."

I couldn't believe I had spoken to Katie that way. I was so angry that I left the house in a spin, slamming the door in Katie's face. I went to Peewee's house and called Don to pick me up. I cried until Don got there. I was so glad to see him and I hugged him so tightly he could hardly breathe. He asked me what was wrong, and I told him about the baby and the fight Katie and I'd had.

"Don't worry. I'll take care of you and our baby," he promised. I was so relieved. By the time we arrived at the house, I was exhausted and fell right to sleep. Katie never came after me, and she never tried to reach me. I wondered why the whole time I was pregnant.

Chapter 7

Don and I got married before the baby was born. I became Mrs. Mekia James Robinson and I had a son, Mich Donald Robinson on February 5, 1979. He was eight pounds, six ounces at birth. Three months after Mich was born, I went back to school to get my diploma. Don and I lived with his mother, and I hated being there because Danielle lived there, too. Ruby helped me with the baby like she was my own mother.

I hadn't expected her to be so generous, and I

wondered how I would ever be able to repay her. Even though I'd had a child with Don and we were married, there was still something about him I couldn't figure out. He never talked about his work, and he and his sister were always arguing about something. When I ask Don what they were arguing about, he just said, "Nothing. Don't worry. That bitch is crazy." I was surprised to hear Don talk about his sister that way, but I let it go.

Mich was six months old by this point, and Katie had not seen him or tried to reach me since our fight. As I sat holding Mich, I started thinking about the irony of how time flies when you're angry at someone you love. As I thought about Katie and how much time had passed, I really began to feel bad. Ruby came into the room and saw me crying. "What is wrong, my child?" she asked.

"My mother and I never made up after the fight we had when I got pregnant," I said. "She has never seen Mich."

Ruby put her hands on my chin, pulling my head up to look at her. She said, "Take the baby to see your mother. You won't rest until it's done." So I took Mich to see his grandmother.

I arrived at Katie's house about 6:30 p.m. with Mich strapped to me. Katie opened the door and began to cry. She hugged me so tightly I thought she was going to crush Mich.

"Let me hold my grandson," she said. "What is his name? He's beautiful." We talked for a long time. We discussed what happened when we found out I was pregnant. I apologized to Katie and she apologized to me. Katie never mentioned why she didn't come after me, and I wondered why she hadn't, but I didn't want to ruin the moment we shared.

By looking around the apartment it was evident that Katie was still doing the same things, but that was her life and I didn't want to interfere with it. Katie had some man named Joe living with her. My sister and brother were not living with her anymore; they were with their daddies. I did not dare ask Katie what had happened. I just knew I wouldn't be spending much time at the place that used to be my home. Joe seemed to be a pretty shady character, just like all the others. As I said good-bye to Katie, I felt very sad. Somehow I knew we would not be seeing a lot of each other. Joe stood behind her in the doorway, smiling like he was up to something and he probably was. I knew I would not be back as long as he was there.

I drove back to the house thinking how happy I was Ruby suggested I take Mich to see Katie. Don was so lucky to have a mom like her. I returned to Don's mother's house around 9:15 p.m. The house was quiet, so I assumed no one was home. I took Mich up to his room and laid him down for the night. I wondered where everyone was. As I started downstairs, I heard a noise. There were voices coming from the other end of the house. As I reached the bottom of the stairs, I noticed the voices were coming from Danielle's room. I moved quietly toward the room, but I couldn't make out what was being said.

As I moved closer to the bedroom door, I could hear Danielle making sex sounds. Bitch. At that point, I decided it wasn't my business who Danielle was having sex with, and I turned around and headed toward the stairs to go back to check on Mich. Just as I got to the steps, the door to Danielle's room opened. I was in shock; it was Don. I ran up the stairs to get Mich.

Don ran after me and caught me before I could get to the room. He grabbed me by the arm and said, "Mekia, you don't understand. She is not my sister." I looked at Don and thought to myself, *He must be out of his mind.*

"It doesn't matter who she is, you were fucking her. How dare you do this to me?" I pulled away from him and continued to go up the stairs. Don continued to come after me. He begged me to listen to him. As I packed my things, I told Don he could go ahead and explain, but whatever he had to say would not stop me from leaving.

He told some bullshit story about how Danielle was blackmailing him into having sex with her. Don continued by saying Danielle had a dirty secret on him and she wouldn't let it go. I asked Don what it was, but he said he couldn't tell me. In a rage, I told Don to go fuck himself. As I started down the stairs, I noticed Danielle standing at the bottom, smiling and wearing a robe. When I reached the bottom of the steps, I put my bag down and put Mich in his car seat. I went back to Danielle and slapped the shit out of her. She stood there stunned, holding her face.

"The next time you decide to fuck someone's husband, try not to get caught," I said. I got Mich and my bag, and headed for the door to leave. Don was standing at the top of the stairs, looking strange. I looked up at him and a tear came from my eye. I thought about Katie.

Lucky for me, I had Aunt Maggie to go to for help.

Aunt Maggie was sixty years old now. It was a pleasure for her to have me there with Mich. Don called every day, begging me to take him back. Deep down in my heart, I wanted to, if for nothing else than he was Mich's father. But I could never forget or forgive him for what he had done to Mich and me. I later found out from Peewee that Don was running drugs for Danielle's boyfriend. Peewee said he didn't know why Danielle was living in the house with Don, but she wasn't Don's sister. I told Peewee something just didn't sound right. I never went back to Don. I spent the next ten years afraid to date or have a relationship with any man. I just did not want to end up like Katie.

Chapter 8

Ten years passed and my Aunt Maggie died. She left me her house and all her possessions. I used the money she left me to go to an accounting school and managed to get a job downtown at an accounting firm. The money wasn't great, but it paid the bills and I had money to put away for Mich to go to college.

I did not keep Don away from Mich. He picked him up every week to visit and bought him things. I never divorced Don, and I never had to put him on child support. Maybe somewhere in the back of my mind, I thought we would get back together one day. He always took care of Mich. I thought about all the years that had passed, but I could never get over how Don had hurt me. I still loved him and I truly believed he loved me, but I couldn't stop thinking if he had done it once, he would do it again. I remained a one-man woman, a virgin to all other men.

Eight more years passed and Mich was eighteen years old, a young man. Katie died that same year. She was found in her house dead from an overdose of heroin. I never would have dreamed in a hundred years Katie would take heroin. I guess that's the price you pay for being green in the hood. I couldn't help but to feel bad about Katie's death. I wish I had spent more time with her and had done more to help her. I wondered for a long time why Katie would turn to using heroin. I never thought she would go that far. I agonized for months over Katie's death. I had no way of contacting my brother or sister after they were taken away from Katie. They did not even attend her funeral. I had no other family left to turn to for comfort. The only one good thing I did have left in my life was Mich.

At eighteen, Mich refused to go to college. He was my pride and joy, and I could not just let him say no to college, but as his father, Don had a much greater influence on him than I did, so I asked Don to talk to him. Of course, he refused to talk to Mich. He just said, "Let him be his own man." After eighteen years, Don still held a grudge against me for leaving him. He wanted me to take him back. I couldn't understand why he was so angry with me. After all, I had caught him in bed with another woman, not the other way around.

Don's grudge against me was so deep; he took Mich under his wing and let him run drugs. How could he do that to his own son?

Don and Danielle now lived in the house alone. I never found out who Danielle's boyfriend was. I guess I didn't care. Don's mother died a year after Katie did. I didn't attend the funeral because I didn't want to see Don and Danielle together. However, I went to her grave later and left flowers on it.

Chapter 9

I had been very depressed about Katie's death and about Mich not wanting to go to college. It was as if I had lost my sense of concentration and left the world for about a week. I totally lost track of time and when I came to my senses, Mich wasn't at home. I looked at the calendar and realized that a week had passed since I had seen him. I checked in his room and saw he hadn't been there. I knew this because his bed was made up and Mich never made his bed. That meant he had not been home since the last time I was in his room.

I called Don several times, but there was no answer. Finally, I decided to go over to Don's house to see if Mich was there. I arrived at Don's house around 7:30 p.m. and knocked on the door. There was no answer, but I continued to knock anyway. Finally it opened very slowly, as if the person behind the door did not want to open it because I was there.

When it was finally open, I was completely surprised to see the man at the door was Johnny. He had aged, but I knew it was him by the scar down the center of his face. I stood there, speechless. I wanted to die right there, but somehow I knew I couldn't let him know I was afraid of him. So, I said, "Johnny, what are you doing here?" I could barely get those words to come out of my mouth.

Johnny stepped out closer to me and said, "I have been here the whole time. I was here when you got pregnant. I was here when you caught Don in Danielle's room. Most importantly, I was here when your poor mother overdosed on drugs. She was so weak for me. I could get her to do anything. You don't think I just left and never saw you or Katie again, do you?" I stood there in shock, wondering what had gone on for all those years in which I thought Johnny was gone.

Johnny continued saying, "You see, Mekia, there was no way I could let you get away with scarring me for life and get nothing out of it. You were a foolish little girl who got her mother to believe her for a moment, until I got her to see things my way. I can't tell you how long I have waited for the day I could tell you what your life has really been about for the last eighteen years. Aha! Aha! Aha!"

I asked Johnny, "What do you mean what my life has been about? What are you talking about?" As I looked at Johnny laughing at me, I instantly knew the past years, in addition to his anger and who knows what else, had turned him into a madman.

I wanted to leave and at the same time, I wanted to feel pity for him, but I couldn't. I had to know if Mich was in the house.

Johnny stood in the doorway staring at me as if he wanted to touch me. All I could think at that time was if he touched me, I would kill him. "Is Mich, my son, here?"

Johnny began to laugh at me again. He made me angry this time. "What are you laughing at, you old fool?" I demanded.

"Fool? Who are you calling a fool? You are the fool who married my son, Don J. Robinson Jr., and the fool who had my grandson, Mich."

I was shattered. It was as if time had gone spinning back to when I first met Don. Now I knew what that something was about Don that I could never figure out. I told Johnny that he was a lying dog. "I don't believe Don is your son. You would say anything to hurt me," I said. "Where is my son, Mich?"

Johnny looked at me and said, "If you want your son, come back to see me tomorrow and we will discuss it." He slammed the door in my face. I stood there banging on the door for what felt like hours, but Johnny never came back.

I drove home blinded by Johnny words, "*You are the fool who married my son, Don J. Robinson Jr.*" Damn, I didn't know what I was going to do. I just knew I had to get Mich away from that madman. *Where was Don? I needed to talk to him.* It seemed like it took me hours to get home. When I finally got there, I sat on my bed for hours, thinking. I thought about Katie and how she used to tell me just to be careful and how she never said anything about Don. I thought about how she pretended to be angry that I was pregnant and how she never talked to Don. I thought about how many times Don and I fucked in my bedroom and how Katie had never said anything to me about it. She must have known what was going on, because she was in the house. She just must have known. Katie had been in on this with Johnny the whole time. She had done it for the drugs. *Damn, being green it the hood ain't no joke.* I sat there thinking about how my own mother had used me for drugs. Ain't that a bitch? The more I thought about Katie and Johnny, the angrier I got. I picked up the phone to try to reach Don on his cell phone, but there was no answer. I got worried because Don always answered his cell phone when I called, no matter where he was. I tossed and turned all night long wondering what Johnny had to say about Mich.

Morning finally came. I said out loud to myself, "Johnny didn't tell me what time to meet him at the house, or was I so upset that I forgot what he said?"

I was starting to get angry with myself when the phone rang. I answered the phone, trying to keep my voice steady and tough. Johnny said, "Good morning, my beautiful daughter–in-law. Have you had your breakfast yet?"

"I don't want to play any games with you," I said. "What do you want and where is my son?"

Johnny replied, "Well, well, you seem to be angry at me."

"Just tell me when to meet you," I demanded.

Johnny replied, "Just meet me at the house in an hour." Then he hung up the phone. I hurried and got dressed in a simple t-shirt, jeans and sneakers.

I arrived at the house at 10:00 a.m. When I rang the doorbell, Danielle came to the door in a red housedress. I looked at her and said, "Where is Johnny?"

In a sexy voice, she replied, "Please come in Mekia. Johnny is expecting you."

I looked at that bitch and thought, *I could kill her right now with no problem or regret. She destroyed my family.* But, it was not her time. My focus was on Mich. The house was different inside; the furniture had been changed, and the walls had been painted a different color. I hated the place; it smelled like Johnny and his cigars. As I sat on the couch waiting for Johnny to come in, I noticed pictures of me, Don and Mich. It was as if Danielle had put me in that room on purpose so I could see them. My stomach began to feel uneasy, but I knew I had to be strong.

Johnny entered the room like he was a king in his castle. I was still afraid of him, but I refused to let him know it. Johnny started the conversation by saying, "Wow, you look great, Mekia."

I thought to myself, *Damn in this shit.*

"I have a grandson, Mich Donald Robinson," he continued. "You never knew my last name, did you Mekia? I made sure of that, y'know. Yes, my last name is Robinson. My full name is Donald Johnny Robinson. It's a great name, isn't it? Now, let's talk about Katie.

Your mother was so damned weak. All I had to do was give her what she wanted and she would do anything I asked. I couldn't have pulled this off without her. Damn dumb ass bitch, may she rest in peace. Hahaha! I certainly hope you didn't inherit her weak traits. I wouldn't want my grandson to be that weak. You see, Mekia, my grandson Mich will take over my dynasty one day. Yes, he works for me, not Don. He is perfect for the role. But, before he can be in charge, I will have to groom him. He will have to do a couple of runs and some other shit for me. He thinks he is going through some sort of initiation stage, but he doesn't know the truth. The truth is, I have arranged for Mich to take on a few special projects for me. He has no idea the shit he will have to endure before he can walk in my shoes. Now, don't get me wrong, Mekia. I love my grandson, but I am still somewhat bitter at you for what you did to me. I don't hate you, because I couldn't have made it this far hating you, but please don't think you can run to Don for help, my dear. Don is dead."

Tears came to my eyes.

Johnny noticed my sadness and said, "Now, now, my sweet, don't cry. Let me tell you something. Don got weak and fell in love with you, and that was not the plan. He was going to come to you, tell you the truth and beg you to leave town with him, just the three of you. I couldn't let him do that. Oh, and by the way, that was not Don having sex with Danielle all those years ago, it was me. Don just happened to come into the room at a bad time. I told him I would kill the baby if he told you the truth. Life stinks, doesn't it, Mekia?"

I sat there looking at the man who had ruined my

life and now wanted to take the only thing I had left in this world. My son. "How could you do this to us?" I demanded.

Johnny just stood there, and then finally said, "Well, I'll tell you Mekia, I can do it very easily. It just gives me a total *rush*."

"What do you want from me?" I pleaded.

"I want you to suffer the way I have suffered. The only thing you can do, Mekia, is wait and see what happens to Mich, and pray I don't kill him. Oh, and Mekia, I hope I don't have to mention the fact that if you even think of calling the police, Mich will surely die, and his body will never be found."

Stunned by his cruel words, I sat there staring at the grotesque scar I had made down the center of Johnny's face. No wonder he had lost his mind. I knew now Johnny had no intention of telling me where Mich was; he only wanted to torment me. I thought to myself, *What can I do to stop him? What can I do to stop him from hurting Mich?* I had to think fast. This was no time to be green. As I sat there thinking about how Johnny had cold-heartedly killed Don and that he could kill Mich as well, I looked over at him and said, "So, Johnny, you want me to suffer. You have my son, you have killed Don, and you helped Katie OD. What more do you think you could possibly do to make me suffer? You have already taken everything away from me. Hell, how do I know you haven't already killed Mich?"

Johnny looked at me, surprised, and said, "True, true. I guess you will just have to wait and see what my next move is. But, I can tell you one thing is for sure. Mich is alive." I stood up from the couch and started for the door, but Johnny grabbed my arm and pressed it tightly. He looked me in the eye and said, "Mekia, I could have made you very happy."

Before I knew what I was saying, I replied, "How could you have done that?" Johnny raised his head back and looked at me, surprised. I stared him directly in his eyes without blinking. Johnny's eyes looked evil, but regretful.

"You could have had all of this and more," he said.

"Why didn't you just come to me after I had grown up? It's like you said, 'I was only a little girl who didn't know what she was doing.' You did say that, didn't you Johnny?" I replied nonchalantly.

"You mean you would have accepted me even after what I tried to do to you?"

I had to think quickly. "Katie told me a bunch of lies about you," I began.

"What do you mean?" Johnny asked.

"Well, Katie told me you were a bad man, and you would try to hurt me. She gave me the knife to put in my bed. She told me you would come into my room one night and I should cut you as hard as I could. I never wanted to cut you, Johnny. She made me do it. Katie also told me that whenever you came around to pretend like I hated you. You see, Johnny, I never really hated you. I wanted you to be a part of our family. You were the best man Katie ever had."

I couldn't believe I had allowed those words to come out of my mouth. Johnny was now looking at me as if in shock. "Are you telling me the truth?" he asked.

"I have no reason to lie to you now," I replied. "I have nothing to gain."

Then he walked over to the window and softly asked, "Is it still too late for us?"

"Well, Johnny, how can I be with you if you are going to hurt Mich?" I replied.

He quickly said, "That can change. All I need to do is make a phone call."

Suddenly, I breathed a sigh of relief. Johnny had just indicated to me that Mich was okay. Now I had to continue to play the game. I questioned myself. Could I actually do this? Damn right I could for the sake of my child. All I knew was that bastard had my son and I had to find a way to stop him. If it meant playing a deadly game with Johnny, then so be it.

I found myself still at Johnny's house after an hour had passed. Johnny had arranged for Danielle to bring us something to eat and drink. I sat there thinking, trying to put the pieces of the game together and decide on my next move. I decided quickly that I needed to get rid of that bitch, Danielle. Johnny seemed to be a lot calmer now, but he had not made the phone call. This meant I still had work to do. Danielle brought sandwiches and two canned sodas for us, but with no ice. I asked Johnny, "Can I have ice with my drink, please?"

He quickly said to Danielle, "Get some ice, you bitch." I was surprised Johnny spoke to Danielle that way, but it assured me he would probably get rid of her if I asked him to. Once Danielle left the room, I said to Johnny, "I've been thinking, Johnny, and to answer your question about whether or not it's too late for us... Well, since you're so successful now, and I need someone to help me with Mich, I would say, no." Johnny looked at me and raised his eyebrow. Then I added, "No! It's not too late for us." Johnny then settled down. "There is one thing, though, Johnny…" I began.

"What is that?" he asked.

"What are you going to do with Danielle?"

He laughed and said, "What do you want me to do with her?"

"Get rid of the bitch. I don't like her," I told him, simply.

"How do I know you will keep your word?" Johnny questioned.

"What do you want me to do to prove to you I am for real? You name it!" Johnny's face lit up with joy and I got sick to my stomach, because I knew what he would ask for. Johnny knew Don was the only man I had ever been with in my life, since he had been there all the time we were together. Yet, somehow it didn't matter. I would do anything to save Mich from Johnny. Johnny was so happy; it was as if he had suddenly changed from an evil, deadly man to a gentle fool.

After we finished our sandwiches, Johnny called Danielle into the room and told her to pack her bags and leave. Danielle looked at me with fire in her eyes. She turned around and left the room without saying anything to Johnny. After she packed her bags, she came back downstairs and said to me, "You will get yours, too, bitch." Then she slammed the door and left. Johnny turned his focus to me.

"Well Mekia, Danielle is gone, just as I promised. Now, this is how you can prove to me you are sincere."

"How, Johnny?" I asked.

"I want you to move in with me tonight," he said, his tone serious.

I was definitely not ready for the deadly game I had gotten myself involved in, but I told Johnny, "Okay, but I will need to get some things from my house."

"No," he said forcefully. "There are plenty of clothes for you here. And you need to call your job and let them know you won't be back to work there."

I looked at Johnny and replied submissively, "Okay." But I knew I would never quit my job. I would call them and request a family leave of absence. A little more time passed, and I asked, "When are you going to make the call to make sure Mich is okay?"

He looked at me and said, "In the morning, and not until then. Mich will be fine, don't worry."

What have I gotten myself into? I worried to myself. *The man I once feared more than anything will now share a bed with me tonight.*

Chapter 10

As night slowly approached, I began to get a little nervous. I had spent the entire day with Johnny, listening as he bragged about his business and what he had accomplished over the years. I had to force myself to keep a straight face, as well as my sanity, and I kept dreading the thought of having sex with him. Maybe since he was old, he wouldn't be able to get it up, and I would be free from doing it with him. Then I thought, *Damn, Viagra.* Johnny talked for what seemed like hours.

It would soon be time for me to play the game with Johnny in bed. My mind swirled with ways to make it through having sex with Johnny. It was around ten and Johnny looked at me the way a man does when he wants to take you to bed.

"Are you sure we should do this?" I asked.

"I have nothing to lose, do you?"

I replied, "Of course not. Let's go upstairs." As I walked up the stairs, I felt as if I was walking into a gas chamber and this was my final march. Johnny walked in front of me, leading the way. I wish I had a knife to stab him in the back, or something to hit him over the head with. Then I remembered that wouldn't do me any good, because then he couldn't make the phone call in the morning to let his people know not to hurt Mich. I was stuck.

When we reached the bedroom, Johnny had a negligee waiting for me on the bed. That damn bed was huge. I had never seen a bed that large except in magazines. Johnny was trying to be very charismatic and gentle. All I could think of was how could I get away with killing him and still save Mich.

His temperature was rising when he said, "See what I got for you to put on?"

"Yes, thank you," I replied, quietly. "It's my favorite color, peach."

"I told you I would take care of you, didn't I?" I took off my clothes and put the negligee on. You could see right through the damn thing. *Just when you thought you had gotten away from the devil, he reappears.*

Even though Johnny was older, he was still very strong. His arms were like iron and his legs were like bricks. I knew he was all man. Don was built the same way. The time had arrived. I tried to prepare myself mentally for what physically unpleasantness lay ahead. Johnny began to get on top of me, kissing me on my neck and rubbing all over my body. He began to caress and suck me in places I never knew existed. I was having sex with my son's grandfather and my husband's father. This was incest in a way a person could never recover from. It was a deadly sin. Johnny slowly started to put his penis inside me and I thought I would die right there in the bed. I wondered if I had done it with him long ago, this might not be happening to me now. But it was happening, and I had to find a way to get through this night and make Johnny think I was all for it. So I relaxed and went with the flow.

For an old man, Johnny really knew how to have sex and make it worth a woman's time. He went for hours having sex with me, on and off, and I wondered what I had gotten myself into. Finally, Johnny had fulfilled his desire to be with me, and he whispered in my ear, "How did you like that?"

I was speechless, until finally I got the energy to say, "That was great, Johnny. I am very impressed." Thinking about what had just come out of my mouth, I wondered if I had really meant it or if I was just pretending. Somewhere in the deep recesses of my mind, I thought I had really enjoyed having sex with him. Keep in mind, however, I had not had sex with a man in eighteen years. As Johnny smiled at me, I couldn't help but stare at the fierce scar on his face. It looked surreal. The whole screwed up situation was surreal. I thought, *Damn, I fucked him up, and I am going to fuck him up again. But this time it will take more than one night.*

So I had made it through the agony of fucking him. Now I had to carefully plan and execute my next move, keeping in mind I would have to be very careful with Johnny because he was not a fool. After realizing he'd enjoyed the sex, I knew one of my weapons against him would be my body. *Damn, if I ain't turning into Katie in the worst way. What a mother does for her child, I mused in my head.*

The next morning, Johnny gave me a bedroom all to myself across the hallway from his room. As I entered the room, I noticed all the colors were my favorites. It was as if Johnny had prepared the room especially for me. The walls were painted eggshell, the bedcovers were peach, and the curtains matched the bedspread. On the bed there were pillows, large and small, just the way I liked them. There was a dresser with pictures of me and Mich arranged on top. The closet was filled with clothes and shoes my size, and designer purses I had always wanted but could never afford. The window was made like a bay window, with a bench sitting area. I loved it. The room was like something from a dream. It was like Johnny had read my mind and knew just how to prepare it. There was one thing that did stand out, however. There was no phone in the room. *Remember, Mekia, you're on a mission to save your son and this is no dream,* I thought to myself. I was entering a world of deadly deception with Johnny, and I knew I had to be very careful.

Chapter 11

As I looked from the bay window in my bedroom, I couldn't help but notice the beautiful day outside. As I sat there, I thought about having sex with Johnny. It sent chills down my body. Was I fantasizing, or did I actually like it? Reality blasted me in the face and I felt nauseous. I had better get to a clinic to get some birth control pills, because it looked like I was going to be having sex with Johnny on a regular basis. I sure as hell didn't want to get pregnant by the bastard.

I was no longer that green little girl he once knew.

Suddenly, a knock on the door startled me. I knew it was the beast. As the door opened, he stood there smiling at me. I had to think quickly, so I moved closer and kissed his forehead. He then pulled me closer and began to kiss me very gently on the lips. *What the hell, there's no turning back now. Let the games begin.* We had sex again, this time in my room. Damn if this old man wasn't full of surprises when it came to sex. I let Johnny have his way with me until I remembered we didn't have birth control. Then I stopped him.

"Johnny, I need to go to the clinic for birth control pills," I said. "At the rate you are going, I hope I'm not too late."

Johnny looked at me and said, "Okay, okay, but would it be so bad to have a child by me?"

"No, it wouldn't be bad, but not right now. We need to get to know each other better, and I need to clear up a lot of bad thoughts Katie put in my mind about you." I tried to sound convincing.

"You're right," he agreed. I was so relieved. Johnny stopped trying to penetrate me, but he continued to perform oral sex like there was no tomorrow. *Damn, that shit feels good.* When we finished having sex, I showered and got dressed. Since I still had work to do on Johnny. I put on the tightest pair of black pants and the lowest cut peach blouse I could find in the closet. I looked in the mirror and thought about Katie, but quickly erased the thought from my mind.

I went downstairs and found Johnny in the large room he called the family room, talking on the phone.

I sat down on the couch and listened to his conversation. He was talking to someone about Mich.

He told the person on the other end to put Mich on the phone, because his mother wanted to talk to him. I breathed a sigh of relief, knowing Mich was alive and safe. Johnny gave me the phone. Mitch was, indeed, on the other end and I quickly asked him if he was all right.

"Yes, Mom. What did you think? I'm traveling to pick up a large shipment, and Johnny has promised to pay me ten thousand dollars for making the run."

"How are you traveling, Mich?"

"By van. Don't worry Mom, because once I get home I'll be able to take care of you and the house."

Just then Johnny grabbed the phone away from me and spoke to someone else. I guessed Mich was riding with someone else in the van and Johnny was controlling the outcome of their trip. Johnny finished his conversation with the man on the phone and then hung up.

"When will Mich be home, and who is he riding with?"

Johnny explained that Mich was traveling across the country in a van with one of his other workers named Baron. "They should be home by the end of the week," he said.

Then I put on a very soft tone, and said, "So Johnny, Mich was never in any danger, was he?"

"No!" Johnny replied, emphatically. "He wasn't, but I had to make sure you'd cooperate with my plan. I knew there was no other way you'd let me show you just how good I could be to you. But don't get me wrong, Mekia. I ain't playin' for nothin'. Remember, I still have someone riding with Mich, and I am calling the shots.

If I tell Baron to kill Mich, he'll do it. It's just a matter of a phone call, like the one I just made. Do you still love me, Mekia? I hope so, because I have a surprise for you when you get back from the clinic."

I made my way to the clinic in the car Johnny had delivered to the house. It was a black 645 BMW. He said it was my car as long as I stayed with him. As I drove toward the clinic, I thought about my next move with Johnny. I wondered if Johnny would really kill Mich, and then I thought about how I had Johnny wrapped around my little finger in bed. I had to figure out how to use what I had to get Johnny to totally trust me. I needed to come up with a plan to get Johnny to tell me all about his business and make him believe I wanted to be a part of his world. "It will take one hell of a woman to make this vicious man weak enough to trust me that much," I said to myself. I had nothing to lose and a world of revenge to gain. Damn, I wanted to get his dick and cut it off.

I bought a supply of birth control pills at the clinic and headed back to the house. As I drove back, I thought about Katie and how she could have used Johnny to make our lives better, but she hadn't. How stupid could she have been? I promised myself I would never be that stupid. Johnny was going to pay for what he had done to my family and me.

I finally stopped daydreaming and decided to go for a little drive to see just what the little 645 BMW could do. As I drove down the highway, I noticed a car following me. I put the pedal to the metal, doing about 90 mph, zipping in and out of lanes. The car following me tried desperately to keep up. I made it to 105 mph and finally got away from the goons. At least I thought I had gotten away.

Damn if it wasn't Johnny's people following me. I got off the highway and decided to drive through the hood to see if Peewee was still around. I really needed someone to talk to. Sure it had been years since I'd seen him, but he still was always someone I could get straight answers from.

As I drove down the street, people started to look at me and point their fingers. I rolled down the window to ask a couple of guys if they knew where Peewee was, and they told me he still lived on top of the hill. Then the guys asked if Johnny was coming down or if he was sending Rocky tonight. I was dumbfounded by their questions, but I had to pretend like I knew what they were talking about.

"I don't know who Johnny's sending, but someone will be down here tonight to take care of you guys." They smiled as I drove off. As I headed for the hill, the strangest thing happened. People on the street waved at me like they knew me. Then I remembered the car. That must be it—they knew the car. Even though it had been quite a few years, when I got to the top of the hill I saw Peewee's place was the same, but without Anna's flowers. I parked the car, went to the door and knocked. The door opened and I saw Peewee, fat as ever.

I gave him a big hug, and he smiled and kissed me on the forehead.

"Damn girl, where have you been? I haven't seen or heard from you since Mich was a little boy. What's up with you, girl? I see you're doing something right, driving a new 645 BMW out the box." I looked at Peewee and started to say something, but my thoughts were interrupted when I noticed the same car that had been following me, pulling in next to the BMW.

"Peewee, do you know who that is?"

"Yeah."

"Well, who is it, fool?" I couldn't believe I yelled at Peewee that way.

He looked sad and said, "That's Johnny's crew. They usually do a lot of his dirty work. That's why he never gets caught doing nothing. That Johnny is a piece of work. But you should know that for yourself, Mekia. The word on the street is you moved in with Johnny, and he put Danielle out. You got it going on girl. Shit, you can have anything you want plus some."

"Word travels fast around here, don't it?" I mumbled to myself.

"Girl, what do you think you're doing with Johnny? That is not your style. You must be desperate for money or something," Peewee interjected.

I didn't respond. Then, after a few moments I said, "Peewee, what do you know about Johnny? Did you know he was Don's father?"

Peewee looked at me funny, and I said, "Don't tell me you knew all along Johnny was playing a game with my life and you didn't tell me."

Peewee looked at me and dropped his head. "I'm sorry, Mekia. Johnny made me promise not to tell you. He threatened to kill me if I told you," Peewee said meekly.

"Well do you work for Johnny then?"

He hesitated and then said, "Uhum."

"That's why nobody in the hood ever bothered you,

right? Because Johnny protected you. Am I right, Peewee?"

Peewee just looked at me and shook his head, and then said, "Yes."

I couldn't believe my ears. The one person I thought I could talk to turned out to be part of Johnny's crew.

I stared him down hard and then said, "You know I am Johnny's lady now, and I can get Johnny to do anything for me. You can trust me, Peewee. I won't let Johnny hurt you. If you need anything, call me on my cell phone." I gave Peewee my cell phone number.

Peewee looked at me with a smile and said, "Thanks, Mekia."

I had to tell Peewee that because I thought he might tell Johnny something I said about him. I hugged Peewee and said good-bye. As I walked to the car, the goons following me were still parked and sitting in their car next to mine. When I started walking toward the car, they drove off in a hurry. While driving back to the house, my mind wandered aimlessly through scenes of my life. *How could this have happened to me? What's really going on? I have to make Johnny pay for his deception.*

Chapter 12

I finally made it back to the house. Johnny's goon squad made sure I got home safely. Johnny was there waiting for me. He must have gotten a report from his goon squad, because as I walked in the door, Johnny said, "So, you finally made it back. Where did you go? You've been gone a long time. I missed you, Peaches."

"Peaches? Who are you calling Peaches?" I asked him.

"That's your new nickname. It goes good with your being my lady."

I informed Johnny I did not like the name Peaches. He looked at me and said, "But peach is your favorite color, so I thought your nickname should be Peaches."

I looked at that fool with fire in my eyes and wanted to tell him to go fuck himself, but I knew I couldn't do that because Mich wasn't home yet. I turned around to look at Johnny and said coyly, "Are you sure you want that to be my nickname?"

"Yes, Mekia. I will call you Peaches," he said.

"Then Peaches it is," I agreed.

I went upstairs to my room and paced back and forth for thirty minutes, thinking. I knew Johnny would be up shortly to check on me. He checked on me often to make sure I was really serious about the relationship. I had to pull myself together before he came upstairs.

Minutes later, Johnny knocked on the door. I let him in and he said, "Peaches, I just wanted to make sure you're okay and ask what took you so long to get back."

I knew Johnny already knew where I was, so I didn't play the fool. "I went by to see an old friend, Peewee. I haven't seen him in years. I didn't stay long, but I did notice something real strange while I was gone. You know, Johnny, people acted like they knew I was your lady now."

"They do know," Johnny smiled wryly. "What's mine is mine. I want people to know you're mine, and if I catch anyone looking at you the wrong way, I'll kill them. Make no mistake, Peaches, I really love you. But if you cross me, I will make you regret it for the rest of your life."

I studied Johnny's face as he spoke. It was eerie. He had a look in his eyes that let me to know he meant every word he said. Johnny turned his back and headed for the door. "Are you coming downstairs to eat dinner with me or not?"

Without any fear of Johnny in my heart, I said, "Yes, I'll be down in a moment. I need to freshen up just a little bit before we eat."

"Very good, Peaches. I'll see you downstairs soon." As Johnny left the room, I stood there thinking, *Let the games begin, Mr. Johnny. I got something for you, too.*

I changed my clothes and went downstairs. Johnny was sitting at the table, reading his paper. You'd think by looking at him, he was a real businessman. Johnny was different from the average drug lord. He never had anyone at his house, he never hung out in the hood, he never did any drugs, and he didn't drive a fancy car. He drove a pick-up truck instead. His ladies were the ones who drove the fancy cars.

Johnny always dressed in black and kept his hair cut short; he wore very expensive cologne and smoked the finest cigars money could buy. As I entered the room, without looking up, Johnny said, "It's good that you could join me, Peaches. I need to talk to you before dinner is served." Johnny had an old Mexican lady who came in, cooked and cleaned house for him.

"What do you want to talk about, Johnny?" I asked, trying to appear interested.

"We need to discuss your future as well as Mich's," he replied.

"What about our future, Johnny?"

"I want to make sure you are okay if something happens to me."

"What do you mean if something happens to you?"

"You know. Anything can happen, and I'm not getting any younger. I have put aside some money just for you, Peaches, in the event something happens to me. There is an account that only my attorney knows about. He will make sure you get the money if something happens to me." Deep down I sensed Johnny wasn't telling me everything, but I decided to let it go for now. At least it gave me something to think about, something to make this living hell worthwhile.

Hmmm. Maybe there's a little something about Johnny's medical history that I can use to Mich's and my benefit, I thought. Dinner was served. We dined on spaghetti with meatballs and a salad; it was delicious. Johnny looked at me with sex in his eyes, and I knew what was up next on the menu. I needed to get dessert off Johnny's mind, so I went to him before he decided to come to me. I put my arms around his neck and kissed him as passionately as I could muster. All the while, I wished I had a knife to slit his throat.

All of a sudden, Johnny picked me up and whisked me upstairs to his room. He grinded on me for hours. I had to give the man credit. He was really good in bed, but damn, I had to get back to my senses. I had to maintain control of the situation.

When he finished with me, he lit a cigar and smoked it in bed. A look of pure satisfaction saturated his every pore. I stared at him, now knowing the more sex I gave him, the more power I would have. It was all a power play, just like he had done with Katie. But, I didn't need drugs to do what I did, or did I? We ended up falling asleep in Johnny's bedroom that night.

Like a groping dog, Johnny woke up in the middle of

the night and wanted me all over again. I gave it to him. Whatever he wanted, I did. The next morning when I awoke, Johnny was not in the bed. I looked around the room and realizing I was alone, I quickly got out of the bed and started to open the bedroom door when I saw Johnny standing there with a tray of breakfast.

"I'm sorry if I scared you, Peaches," he said. "I went down and had this made for you. You were sleeping so soundly that I didn't want to bother you. Get back in bed and eat your breakfast, you sweet thang."

I got back in bed and ate a little bit of the food. Johnny sat there looking at me like he had never seen me before.

"Why are you looking at me that way?" I asked.

He said in a low voice, "I think I am falling in love with you, Peaches."

I coughed a little and said, "What are you saying, Johnny?"

"When I first told you to move in with me, I had no idea I would be swept away like this," he confided. "Now I know why Don fell in love with you so easily. Your sweetness is irresistible."

I was speechless. Then I thought about Don and asked Johnny, "When did you kill Don?"

Johnny got very upset at my question and began yelling at the top of his lungs, "Why are you asking about Don? I am your man now! Me, not Don."

He was furious. Johnny left the room, slamming the door as he left. I sat there in the bed, confused about what had just happened. Now, what had I done?

Two days passed, and Johnny didn't say anything to me. I knew I had to fix whatever the problem was.

The only way I knew how was to sex him, so I went to him dressed in a red bra, matching thong and red heels. Johnny was in his office talking on the phone with someone.

I entered the room, walking backward so he could see my ass first. Johnny quickly hung up the phone. Slowly I sauntered toward him and sat in his lap. I turned toward him and wrapped my legs around him. I wanted him to feel my heat pumping, so I started kissing him, and in a soft voice, I let him know I was sorry for what happened. "I belong to you, Johnny, and only you," I whispered. I was so good, I even fooled myself. I made Johnny have sex with me in the chair.

Even though it had been eighteen years since my pussy had any action, I was really beginning to get good at the sex game. An eerie vision clouded my eyes as I saw myself turning into Katie. I began to feel like a prostitute playing a deadly game of survival. When we finished having sex, Johnny was spent, but I could tell by his smile, he wasn't mad at me anymore. I was happy I'd done what I did. Johnny thought he had me right where he wanted me, but I had to make sure the joke would be on him. I went upstairs to shower and change, and later came back downstairs to get the game plan on Mich's arrival home the next day.

"So, Mich will be home tomorrow," I said, smiling at Johnny. "What time?"

Johnny looked at me with seriousness in his eyes and said, "There's been a change of plans."

"What change of plans?" I asked cautiously.

"Well, something came up and I was forced to send the guys in another direction," Johnny explained.

"What do you mean?" I asked, trying not to sound impatient.

"There was word on the street the van Mich and Baron was in was going to be hijacked, so I called Baron and told him to head north until I let him know when to come back this way."

"What about Mich, Johnny? Is he safe?" I pleaded for answers.

"Mich is okay. He understands the risks associated with this game, Peaches."

"But how do I know Mich is really okay?" I protested.

Johnny looked at me and said in a strong voice, "You don't, but I assure you he is okay. I thought you had grown to trust me by now."

"I do trust you, but I need to know that Mich is okay, Johnny. Please call him right now and let me talk to him." Johnny looked put off as he picked up the phone, but he relented. He dialed the number, gave me the phone and left the room.

"Mich, dear, are you okay?" I asked, trying not to let him hear the panic in my voice.

"Mom, what are you worried about? Let me be a man. I know what I'm doing. Johnny has taught me a lot and I promise I'll be okay. But please, mom, you can't call me like this because you never know what I might be into. I won't be home for a couple of weeks, or longer. Johnny told us to lay low for a little while until things quiet down. Danielle must have ratted on us."

"How do you know about Danielle, Mich?" I asked.

"Mom, Johnny tells me everything."

"What do you mean, Johnny tells you everything?"

"I know about Danielle, I know about Dad's accident, and I know Johnny is in love with you. I sure am glad Johnny told you about Dad's accident, because I didn't want to have to tell you," Mich said.

"What do you know about your dad's accident, Mich?" I asked.

"Well, Johnny told me Dad got into a shootout with a group of guys in a club. Johnny told Dad not to go, but Dad didn't listen to him."

"Oh, I see," I replied. "And what do you know about Johnny, Mich?"

"Mom, come on. Johnny is the man. He told me you moved in with him. I'm really glad to hear it. Now I can do what I need to do here and make sure things get done right for Johnny."

"Is that all you know about Johnny, Mich?" I prodded.

"What else is there to know? He's a cool guy. Mom, you should be happy. He cares so much about you. I know Johnny cannot take Dad's place, but he has done a lot for me."

"Okay, Mich. I guess I will let you go now. I'll see you when you get back. Be safe."

"Good-bye, Mom."

I could not continue the conversation with Mich any longer. He sounded like a brainwashed punk. I never thought I would hear my son talk that way. I began to think about the situation. Something wasn't right. Either Mich didn't know Johnny was his grandfather or Johnny was lying to me about everything. I was more confused than ever. Was Johnny telling me the truth about being Don's father, or did he make that shit up?

Did Johnny really have Don killed, or what? How could I get to the truth?

Chapter 13

Johnny stayed away from me that night. He must've known Mich told me things that made me wonder, and he was right. I couldn't sleep. I knew Johnny was full of tricks, but it was time for me to get to the bottom of things. I had to take a chance with Johnny. I cleaned myself up, put on Johnny's favorite perfume and the peach, see-through gown, and went to Johnny's room. I knocked on the door and he said, "Come in."

I opened the door and found Johnny sitting on his bed reading. For a damned drug dealer, he sure did a lot of reading.

I crawled onto the bed and said, "Mich doesn't know you're his grandfather, does he?"

Johnny didn't say anything. "Come on, Johnny. You've got to tell me the truth," I pleaded. "I thought we were trying to get to know and trust each other. How can we do that if you don't tell me the truth?"

"Okay, Peaches, you got me. You're right. I haven't told Mich about me. I cannot tell him how I became his grandfather. He would never understand. You must promise me never to tell him either. Do you understand me?" Johnny put his hands around my neck and pressed hard.

When I began to cry, he stopped. He removed his hands from my neck and said, "Peaches, I'm sorry. I didn't mean to scare you. I don't know what came over me. It's just that when I think about my grandson knowing what kind of a monster I was ... I ... I ... I don't know, it does something to me."

Right at that very moment I knew Johnny's second weakness was his grandson. *Why was Mich one of Johnny's weaknesses?* I wondered. I sat there on the bed, holding my neck and pretending Johnny had really hurt me, rubbing it gently and making myself cry. I wanted to see if I could get next to Johnny and make him regret hurting me, but it didn't work out like I planned. Johnny became angry and told me to get out of his room. Something else must have made him mad, but what? I ran out of his room in fear.

Things were starting to unravel. I didn't have my game on. Things with Johnny were coming at me from all directions. The next morning, I stayed in my room thinking of my next move. I was figuring maybe a new hairstyle might brighten my spirits, so I started to get ready. Looking in the closet for something to wear, I picked out a really cute red dress with matching red shoes. Once I was ready to go, I heard a knock on the door. "Come in, Johnny," I said. He stood there in the doorway, looking at me with a crazy look.

"Peaches, I want to apologize to you for my behavior yesterday. I was totally out of place. Will you forgive me?" he asked.

I looked at that damned fool and said to myself, *Work it, Peaches.* Then I said, "Sure Johnny, that's what people in love do, they forgive each other."

The look on Johnny's face changed immediately when he heard me mention that four-letter word.

"Peaches, did you just say you love me?" he asked, incredulously.

"Yes, as a matter of fact, I did!" He grabbed me and kissed me really hard on the lips, apparently very happy with my response.

Suddenly he brightened up. "I forgot about the surprise I have for you, Peaches."

"What surprise, Johnny?" I smiled.

"You remember I told you I had a surprise for you the day when you went to the clinic?"

"Oh, yeah. What is it, Johnny?"

"Well, I have business in New York, and I want to take you with me. You can shop while I handle my business. How does that sound to you, Peaches?"

I was in shock. New York. I never thought in a hundred years I would be going to New York ... or anywhere else for that matter. I had never been out of the State of Georgia.

"Yes, yes, Johnny. I want to go with you," I said, bursting with enthusiasm. Johnny then eyed me up and down, noticing the red dress and heels.

"Where are you going dressed like that, Peaches?"

"I thought since you were angry with me, I'd go to the hair salon to get a new hairdo," I replied.

"Well I'm not mad at you anymore. How long will it take?"

"Maybe two or three hours, depending on the crowd," I replied.

"Okay, but make sure you're back before dark. Don't make me come looking for you, girl. You look too damn good in that dress. Matter of fact, you look good enough to eat right now."

I quickly said, "Now Johnny, if I let you do that, I will never get to the hair salon."

He looked confused, but obliged. "Okay, I was just playing with you. Get out of here and hurry back." I hurried to the BMW and quickly took off. Damn, I was glad to be out of that house and away from Johnny.

Strange as it may seem, I was starting to believe my name really was Peaches, since I had heard it so much over the past few weeks. "Damn, that bastard is crazy," I said to myself as I drove. "I have to find a way to get away from him. Maybe once we go to New York, I will be able to think things through more clearly." Mich wouldn't be back for several weeks and I needed to find a way to re-group. Having sex with Johnny every day was driving me crazy in more ways than one. I knew I didn't like him, but I loved the sex. However, the game was to get in and get Mich out, and it wasn't as easy as I thought it would be. Now, I had to go deeper. I had to go deeper into Johnny's world of drugs, lies, murder and deception.

I finally got to the hair salon and was happy to find it wasn't crowded. Drew, the hairdresser, was gay, and he knew how to do some hair. He asked me what I wanted him to do. I really didn't know, so I told him to do whatever he thought would look good on me. I knew I was in good hands. My hair was very long, and I always wore it up in a French roll, but Drew was the perfect person to give me a new look. After he finished, he gave me the mirror, stood in front of me and said, "Now Mekia, why did you wait so long to come and see me, girlfriend?" Then he said, "Feast your eyes on this masterpiece." I looked into the mirror, and to my surprise, there was a beautiful, young woman who could really be named Peaches.

Drew had done a great job on my hair. He left it longer, put gold streaks in it, and feathered it back the way the stars and white girls wear their hair. I couldn't believe my eyes. I felt so good looking at myself. This was the first time in my life I could really say I looked great. With my new hairdo, red dress and heels I had on, I felt like I had turned into a new person. I got into the BMW and sped off. I decided to test my looks out, something I never would have done in the past, so I went to a bar on 5th Street in downtown Atlanta.

Of course Johnny's goons followed me, but I didn't try to lose them this time. As good as I looked, I wanted some protection. I got to the bar, parked the BMW in front, and walked in the front door. All eyes were on me. *Damn. Is this what I've being missing all this time?* I thought. I sat at the bar and ordered a dirty martini. The bartender couldn't keep his eyes off me. Then I noticed a man approaching me. He was tall, with a medium build, and he looked like he was of Italian descent. He had jet-black hair and spoke with a slight accent.

"How are you madam, this lovely evening?"

"Fine," I replied.

"May I buy your drink?"

"Sure, have a seat." He introduced himself as Art.

"What is your name?"

"You can call me *Peaches*," I said in a sexy voice. As I talked to Art, I noticed Johnny's goon squad in the back, looking at me and taking notes for Johnny. Art was a mild-mannered man, but I could tell he had been around. In other words, he was a well-seasoned man with a lot of character. I stayed at the bar for an hour talking with Art. When I noticed the time, I told him I had to be going. Art asked if he could call me sometime.

"Yes, sure, why not," I answered nonchalantly. *Why did I do that? If Johnny finds out, he'll kill me. Oh, what the hell*, I mused to myself as I gave him my cell phone number. I told him to call me, let it ring once and hang up, and I'd call him back later. Gee, a girl's gotta live now and then. It had been eighteen years and I'd been cooped up looking like an old bag! Art and I talked for a little while longer and then I told him I had to go. He looked at me like he wanted to rip my clothes off, and I knew I'd better get out of there.

He kissed my hand and I left the bar, practicing a walk to die for. It must have worked, because every man in the bar, including the ones with dates, stopped to look at me. When I got to the car, voices in my head

taunted me. *I shouldn't have given him my cell number.*
I tried to quiet the voices by saying to myself, "What the
hell, Johnny doesn't own me. Fuck him." Big words.

When I got home, it was dark, and suddenly I remembered how Johnny had told me to get home before
dark. He was probably going to be pissed off. "I'm not
going to let him control my every move," I said as I tried
to comfort myself. "Shit I am not a child," I told myself. When I opened the door, Johnny was sitting on the
couch waiting for me. He was angry until he saw me
and my new hairdo. Then he quickly changed his expression. "Damn, you look like a perfect jewel, and you
belong to me," he said.

"Sorry I'm a bit late in the dark, Johnny, I decided to
get me a drink before I came home. You know, I wanted
to be ready for you. Making me get home before dark is
stressin' me, Johnny. You gotta cut me some slack."

Johnny looked at me strangely and said, "I guess
you're right. But don't try anything. I have people in
place and I'm not fooling around with you, Peaches."

"I know baby, I know," I said.

His words made me feel a little bit frightened,
especially since I had just given an Italian my cell phone
number. Johnny picked me up and ran upstairs. I never
saw a man get up a flight of stairs so quickly. He rushed
me to the bed and the rest is history. He tried to sex me
all night long until he couldn't function anymore. I fell
asleep in his bed and awoke in the middle of the night.
Johnny was still sleeping and I thought to myself, *I
could kill this fool right now, and he would never know
what hit him.* But then I thought, *I look too good to go
to jail.* I quietly left Johnny's bed and went to my room.

I thought about Art and wondered if he would call me. *He's an Italian; they don't date black women, do they?* I fell back to sleep thinking about going to New York.

The next morning, Johnny was up and moving about. I could hear him whistling a happy tune. I was packing for the trip when he came into my room and said, "You don't need to pack. Whatever you want, I will buy it for you."

I thought to myself, *Damn, if I could only get him to bring Mich home.* I stopped packing, grabbed my designer purse and went downstairs to wait for the limo.

Chapter 14

We arrived in New York City at 2:15 p.m. There was plenty of daylight left to see the city and shop. Johnny had a limo waiting for us outside the airport. When I got into the limo, I looked at Johnny, and for a moment, I was speechless. I sat there wondering, *What the hell am I doing here with this man? Am I playing the game or am I loving every moment of this shit?* Then I felt Johnny shaking me on the arm. He was calling me, "Peaches, Peaches, Peaches."

"Oh, oh, I'm sorry. I was in a daze thinking about being here in New York with my man," I cooed. That was all Johnny needed to hear. Those words put a big smile on his face.

Johnny paged the driver and told him to take us to the hotel. He had made reservations at the Waldorf Hotel. When we pulled up to the hotel, I looked out of the window and saw what I thought was a castle. "This place must have cost an arm and a leg. Can we afford to stay here, Johnny?"

He looked at me and laughed. I became embarrassed, and he knew it. He grabbed my hand kissed it and whispered, "Peaches, nothing in this world is too good for you."

I looked into his eyes, and I knew I was in deep shit. I didn't say anything else until we got to the room. Secretly I was hoping Johnny had reserved two rooms, but I had no such luck. There was only one room for both of us, but it was beautiful. I thought I was in a dream world when I got inside. I couldn't believe people really lived like this. Johnny gave the bellman a tip and he left.

Johnny stood in the doorway looking at me with that crazy look again.

"Why are you looking at me that way?" I asked.

"Because you are much more beautiful than I ever imagined you to be," he said.

I acted like a schoolgirl and giggled. "Oh, stop it, Johnny."

"Can I sex you now or later?" I looked at him, but didn't know how to reply. "Okay, I know you want to go shopping."

I was relieved to hear him say that. "Does it show that bad?" I asked.

"Yes, it does. Here, take this money and have the limo driver take you wherever you want to go."

"But Johnny, I don't know where to go. Remember, I've never been to New York before."

"Oh yeah, yeah. I'll make sure the driver takes you to the best of the best."

I got into the limo and the driver took off. We arrived at a place with several stores. I went in and browsed around, looking at the most beautiful dresses and accessories I had ever seen, but I couldn't concentrate on what to buy because I was thinking about the mess I had gotten myself into with Johnny. The game wasn't as easy as I thought it would be, and I definitely needed some help. But whom could I trust?

Despite my temptation to indulge myself, it was hard for me to keep my mind on shopping when I knew I was becoming deeper and deeper involved with a madman—a man who obviously had enough money to do anything or buy anybody he wanted to. I, on the other hand, was a stupid fool who thought she could outwit a man like Johnny. But I had no idea he was that powerful. Just look at what he had done. He had changed my name to Peaches, and I let him. He had sex with me any time he wanted to. And he still had my son. What should I do? Should I leave and take a chance he would find me and kill me, or should I stay and play the hand I had been dealt? If I tried to leave, he would find me.

Suddenly another voice collided within my mind. It was loud and strong. It forced me to listen to it, as it said, *I don't know any man who would let a woman leave after what Johnny has done. Since my name is Peaches, I need to become Peaches.*

Just then I felt someone's hand on my shoulder. I turned around and saw it was Art. "Hello, madam Peaches," he said.

"Art from Atlanta, right?"

"Yes. What are you doing here in New York, Ms. Peaches?"

"Oh, just shopping," I replied.

"Are you married, Ms. Peaches?"

"No. I'm here in New York with a friend," I told him. "Are you married?"

"No."

"A good-looking man like you isn't married?" I flirted.

"I was married once, but it didn't work out," he explained.

"Yes, I know what you mean. I was married once myself, and it didn't work out for me either."

Art smiled and said, "Would you have dinner with me tonight?"

"Well, I can't have dinner, but maybe we can have a drink before I go back to my hotel," I tried to appease him.

Art smiled and said, "That sounds great."

"I am in a limo. Are you driving?" I asked.

"Are you kidding? Driving here in New York? Heck no," he replied. "There is a bar across the street. We can go there if you like." We left the shop and headed for the bar. It was nice and cozy, and there were lots of people talking.

Art asked if I wanted to sit at the bar or a table. "A table will be fine." I choose the table because I could see the door just in case I needed to hide. Art helped me with my seat and then he sat down.

"I'm so very surprised to see you here in New York. I thought it was you. I just couldn't leave the store without saying something to you. I have called you several times on your cell, but you haven't responded."

"Well, I couldn't get away from the man I am involved with. You must understand those things?"

"Are you in love with this man you are with?"

"No, I am not. He has something that belongs to me, and I want it back. The only way I know how to get it, is to give him what he wants," I said matter-of-factly.

Art looked at me and said, "And what does he want from you?"

"You know, what all men want. Sex."

"You shouldn't have to do that. Why don't you just ask him to give you what you say is yours."

"It's not that easy, Art."

"What do you mean, it's not that easy. Have you tried to ask him?"

"Yes."

"Well, what did he say?"

"It's a long story, Art. And it would take me too long to explain it to you. Besides, I must get back to the hotel. He'll be waiting for me."

Art looked at me and said, "I tell you what. Take my card and call me if you need anything. If you just need to talk, call me."

I looked at him, smiled and said, "Thanks. I'll do that, Art."

I got up from the table and walked away. As I walked back to the store where I was shopping, I turned around, but Art was gone. I looked at the card he had given me:

ART. Call me if you need me. 555-555-1234. I put the card in my purse and went back inside the store. I bought five dresses and shoes to match. Then I got in the limo and told the driver to take me back to the hotel.

When I arrived back at the hotel, Johnny was on the phone yelling at someone. It was obvious someone had messed something up. I grabbed my bags and went into the bedroom. I could still hear Johnny yelling. He made several other calls and the conversations seemed to last for hours. I couldn't make out what was going on, as Johnny even spoke in another language. I tried to listen to as much as I could, but I wasn't getting anywhere. If only I could hear what the other person was saying on the other end.

I looked over at the phone on the table in the bedroom and thought, *Should I pick up the phone and listen? Hell, yes. It's time I get more information about what Johnny is up to.* I picked up the phone quietly, and I was surprised to hear the person on the other end was a female. Johnny may have been yelling, but she was the person in charge.

From what I could hear, Johnny was trying to explain to her what had happened to a shipment that didn't show up last month. The van was detoured up north because someone was trying to set him up. The woman told Johnny to make it right or she would send someone who could make it right. I didn't like the sound of her threat, so I quickly hung up the phone.

I could hear Johnny in the other room. He was still very angry and smashed a glass into the fireplace and broke it. *I hope he don't come back here with that shit,*

I thought. Johnny paced up front for a while before he finally came into the bedroom.

"Peaches, did you enjoy your shopping trip?" he asked.

"Yes, Johnny, thank you so much," I tried to sound appreciative. Then I asked, "Is everything all right with business?"

"Well, to tell you the truth, there is a problem. We need to get back to Atlanta right away."

"So when are we leaving?"

"First thing in the morning. Our flight leaves at eight."

"Is everything okay?" I asked.

"It will be once I get back to Atlanta," he replied.

Chapter 15

We arrived back in Atlanta around ten. Johnny had a limo waiting for us at the airport. As we rode back to the house, Johnny was eerily quiet. I could tell he had something hard pressing his mind. I wondered if I should ask him if there was anything I could do to help, but I hesitated because I didn't know how he would react.

I was beginning to see just how strange Johnny was. You had to approach him at the right time, otherwise he might bite a hole in your ass. I decided not to say anything to him. Then, my cell phone started ringing. I looked at the number and it was my job calling me.

Johnny said, "What, are you going to answer the phone or are you hiding something from me?" I answered the phone.

The voice on the other end said, "This is Carol calling from the Atlanta Accountant Firm. We are calling to let you know your family leave has expired."

"I don't know why you are calling me, because I won't be coming back there to work. I thought I made that clear to you when I left. I have a husband who takes care of me and I don't need to work. Please don't call me again." I hung up the phone. Then I added for my final sales pitch, "Damn job makes me sick."

"Are they trying to get you to come back?" Johnny asked.

"Yes, but you heard what I told them, didn't you?"

With a big smile on his face, he replied, "Yes, I heard what you told them." Then he kissed me on my cheek.

I thought to myself, *Damn, I got out of that one.*

We finally made it to the house around 10:30 a.m. I could tell it was going to be a beautiful day. The sun was shining and there was a slight breeze. As the limo drove up, I saw there was a car parked on the street in front of the house. Johnny looked out the window with a concerned look on his face.

"What's the matter, Johnny?"

"Nothing for you to be concerned with." We got out of the limo. The limo driver popped the trunk, and Johnny quickly went to help the driver with the bags. He grabbed two bags and walked toward the house, carefully looking around as he walked. I was behind

JUST WHEN YOU THOUGHT

Johnny and the driver was walking beside me.

As we approached the door, Johnny stopped and looked back again. Then he got his keys out of his pocket and opened the door. He stood there and motioned for me to go inside. Johnny came inside next, then the driver. Johnny gave the driver a tip and the driver left, but Johnny stayed in the doorway watching all the while. I couldn't help but ask, "Are you okay, babe?"

"Yes, Peaches, I'm fine. Everything is fine," he said as he closed the front door.

I took off my shoes and started upstairs when the doorbell rang. I stopped halfway up the stairs. Johnny looked up at me with a concerned look on his face, then went to the door and looked out the peephole.

He relaxed, looked up at me and said, "It's okay, it's okay." His voice sounded like that of a man who was totally relieved from serious concern. Johnny opened the door and said, "What are you two doing here so soon?"

I was anxious to know who was at the door, so I started back down the stairs. As I reached the last step, a man came in with a bald head, wearing jeans, a white T-shirt, and a gold chain around his neck. *Who in the hell is that?* I wondered. *No one ever comes to see Johnny.* Then, to my surprise, another man came in the front door. It was Mich. He had lost some weight, but he was as handsome as ever. I ran to Mich and hugged him, kissing him on his forehead. I was so happy to see him that I almost cried. Mich embraced me; he was happy to see me, too. He had a big smile on his face. Johnny stood there looking at me with jealousy. *What's wrong with that fool? This is my son.*

Johnny quickly broke our contact with each other

by saying, "Mich, let your mom go upstairs and change. We just got back from New York and she's tired."

I was nowhere near tired. I looked at Johnny and rolled my eyes at him in a sneaky way. That fool was up to something. I went upstairs to shower and change as quickly as I could. When I got back downstairs, Johnny, Baron, and Mich were in the den talking. Someone had left the door cracked, which was good, because I could hear what was being said.

Mich was talking, and he said, "Uncle Johnny, don't be upset with us."

Johnny said, "What, what?"

"We had to leave the shipment behind," Mich said.

Johnny yelled, "What?"

"Now, wait, Uncle Johnny. Let me explain what happened before you blow up. Baron and I left the hotel to go get some lunch and when we came back, the hotel was surrounded by cops. So, Baron and I turned around and left to come back here. We tried to reach you, but you didn't answer your cell phone. Baron made sure the cops couldn't trace us; he gave the hotel a fake ID. With the cops on a stakeout, we had to leave the entire shipment in the room."

Johnny looked like he had seen a ghost. He turned and went to the window. Looking out the window, he said, "Damn, who is doing this to me? Who? When I find out who is doing this, they're dead."

"Who do you think it could be?"

"I don't know, but someone is playing me too close."

"Could it be Danielle?" Mich asked.

Johnny turned from the window and said, "Maybe. I will find out today."

Baron was sitting in the big, high-back chair. He crossed his legs and asked Johnny, "So, Big J. Why did you come back from New York so soon? I thought you would be there until next week."

"I had to cut the trip short because I received a call from Camilla."

Baron uncrossed his leg and said, "Camilla? The madam?"

"Yes, she called me while I was in New York complaining how someone sent word to her that I was stealing money from her. After all these years of dedication, she has some nerve calling me to accuse me like that. How could she believe anything like that?"

I remained near the door, listening to the conversation and wondering, *Who in the hell is Camilla?*

Johnny was still talking. He said, "Somebody is trying to throw some shit into my game and it's making Camilla very, very unhappy. In this business, you don't want to make the madam unhappy. It could mean your life."

Mich asked Johnny, "Who is Camilla the madam?"

"Camilla is the head man in charge of the cartel."

"Where is she?" Mich asked.

"In Italy, and she is nobody you want to mess with. Trust me, son."

"What does she want you to do, Uncle Johnny?"

"That's why I had to come back from New York early. I have to get my books to her before the end of today. That's how I'm going to prove to her I'm still straight," Johnny said.

"Are you sure, Uncle Johnny?" Mich asked.

"Yes, son, no doubt about it."

"Uncle Johnny, this sounds just like Danielle. You know she can be a bitch when she is angry at someone."

"I know. I did do her wrong by putting her out like that after all these years. But, what could I do? Your mom wanted to move in with me."

"Why did Mom all of a sudden want to move in with you?" Mich asked.

"Well, she was pretty upset when I broke the news to her about your dad, so she stayed over that night. After that, she asked if she could move in."

"That sure doesn't sound like Mom. You mean you slept with her that night, Uncle Johnny?"

Johnny turned away from Mich so he could not see his face, and said, "What can I say? The old man still's got it."

I was still standing outside the door listening to that lying bastard. *He can lie like a dog to save his ass. I wonder if he really is stealing money from this Camilla.*

"Now, enough of this talk. Let's get back down to business."

"Okay, Uncle Johnny," Mich replied like a brain-washed fool.

"There have been two episodes against me and my operation to make me look bad. I don't know if I can survive another one. The first thing I need to do is find Danielle and question her."

Baron looked at Johnny and asked, "Do you know where the bitch is, Big J?"

Johnny turned around and said, "Yes, as a matter of fact, I do. I always keep my enemies close to me." Johnny sat down in his big, high-back, black chair. He lit a cigar and said, "This is what I want you to do, Baron. Call Tommy and Rock, and you'll go to this address." He wrote something down on a piece of paper and gave it to Baron. It must have been Danielle's address. "Bring that bitch back here to me right away," Johnny said.

"What about Mekia, Johnny?"

Johnny jumped up from his chair, pulled out a knife and pressed it to Baron's neck. "Don't you ever call her Mekia again! Her name is Peaches! You fucking got that?"

Baron looked flat out at Johnny with a look that said, "I ain't afraid to die." Then he said, "God damn, Big J. It won't happen again, man. I didn't know you changed her name."

Johnny pulled away from Baron and said, "Don't worry about Peaches. I'll take care of her. She won't be here when you bring Danielle back."

Mich stood back from Johnny and asked, "Uncle Johnny, what do I call Mom?"

Johnny said to Mich, "She is your mom. You call her Mom anyway, don't you?"

Mich said, "I guess so."

Johnny sat back down in his chair and said, "Okay, let's get this thing moving."

"What about me, Uncle Johnny?"

Grinding his teeth, he said to Mich in a stern voice, "Stop calling me goddamn Uncle Johnny. You sound like a little bitch. If you are going to play in this game, you've got to be a real man. Call me Big J."

Mich sat quietly and didn't respond. Then he said, "Okay, Big J. What do you want me to do to help?"

Johnny sat back in his chair and said, "That's better, Big M. You can take your mom out to lunch and keep her gone until I call you. Here, take this cell phone. It's yours now."

Johnny started to leave the room. Then he turned and said, "And by the way Mich, don't let your mom talk you into going anywhere after you eat. You got that, Big M?"

Mich gave Johnny a small smile and said, "Got it, Big J."

Johnny saw the hurt expression on Mich's face and knew he'd have to fix that. He went back over to Mich and gave him a "you are the man" handshake and said, "Mich, this means a lot to me. Don't let me down, okay?"

Mich gave Johnny the smile he was looking for and said, "You can count on me, Big J."

I saw Johnny getting ready to come out of the room, so I quickly took off my shoes and ran as fast as I could up the stairs. I couldn't let Johnny catch me listening to his conversation. Just as I reached the top of the stairs and turned around, Johnny looked up at me and said, "Peaches, dear, you look as refreshed and lovely as ever." I put my shoes down and started to put them on. I had changed into a slinky dress and Johnny was gazing at my legs.

"Guess what, Peaches?"

"What, babe?"

"Mich wants to take you to lunch. Isn't that great?"

"Good, that will give me a chance to see where his head is."

"Well, I guess I can let you go for a little while since

he's your son." Johnny looked at me funny and added, "But, before you go, let me give you a little something." Johnny came upstairs and grabbed my arm. He turned around and looked down at Mich and Baron and said, "You guys can wait in the den for me. I'll be right back." He then led me to his bedroom. Once we got to the bedroom, Johnny faced me squarely and said, "Now Peaches, don't be stupid and try to tell Mich anything you'll regret."

"What are you talking about, Johnny?"

"You know exactly what I'm talking about. Just don't tell Mich anything about me, you got that?"

I turned my back to him and said, "Yeah, I got it." He forcefully grabbed me by my arm and turned me around to face him. Then he playfully started kissing me.

"I didn't get a chance to sex you the way I wanted to in New York. You do know that, don't you?"

"Yes, I know," I answered. Then I thought about how he reacted to Baron and Mich downstairs in the den, so I decided to let Peaches come back out. "So what are you going to do about it, Big J?" I teased.

He looked at me and turned around to lock the bedroom door, something he never did, then he pushed me on the bed and took my clothes off. He sexed me for thirty minutes. Afterward, he said, "That's just a taste of what you'll get later tonight."

I looked at him with pleasure in my eyes and said, "I can't wait."

Johnny got up with a smile on his face and said, "I got business to take care of. Do what you got to do and I will see you later." He slammed the door, and I got dressed to go eat lunch with my son.

When I got downstairs, Johnny was on his cell phone pacing the floor. Mich and Baron stood up when I entered the room. "You really look good, Ms. Peaches," Baron said.

Mich added, "Yeah Mom, you do look great. Being with Big J has changed you."

If only you knew how much, I said to myself, but out loud I said, "Maybe it's the hairdo." Johnny had left and gone down to the basement. I told Baron to tell him we were leaving and motioned for Mich to come on. When we got to the car, Mich's face burst into a smile.

He said excitedly, "Mom, Big J's got you riding good, don't he?"

"Yeah, yeah. Get in the car." I took off really fast thinking how happy I was to be out of the house, away from Johnny and with my most precious son.

Chapter 16

The car had pick up. I'd sure give it that. I didn't notice how fast I was going until Mich said, "Mom, do you know how fast you're going?"

I looked at the speedometer and saw I was doing over 100 mph. Mich said, "Don't get me wrong; I like going fast, but not with my mom."

"You're right. Thanks for keeping me honest, Mich." I felt so comfortable at that very moment, as if this nightmare was just that—make-believe. My mind actually went into fast forward thinking, *Now that*

I have Mich back safe, I can leave Johnny. I've got to make our plan. "Where do you want to eat, honey?" My thoughts were interrupted.

"Let's go to the Steakhouse. I haven't had a good meal since I left Atlanta." As I drove, I thought about the conversation I had overheard Johnny, Baron and Mich having at the house. Johnny really had Mich brainwashed. *How can I break through that wall? He's a fool for Johnny, thinking he's a great man. This is an obstacle I didn't expect.*

Since Mich had the stereo blasting, I couldn't really talk to him in the car, so I decided to wait until we got to the restaurant.

We finally reached the Steakhouse and the hostess took us to our table. After we sat down, I looked directly into Mich's eyes. He was so handsome, just like his father. I wanted to cry, but I didn't. I thought about Don and how happy we used to be. *I don't know if Don was happy or not. He was just following Johnny's instructions. Johnny said Don was going to tell me the truth and ask me to leave town with him, but I can't believe anything Johnny says.* Then I snapped out of it. Mich was talking to me. "Mom. Mom, you didn't hear a word I just said, did you?"

"I'm sorry, honey. I was daydreaming."

"That's easy to do when you got a man like Big J showering you with anything you want."

"Will you please stop? Just stop!" I exclaimed. The other people in the restaurant turned to look at me. I didn't realize how loud I was. In a lower voice, I said to Mich, "I'm sorry, baby, but will you please stop putting Johnny on this pedestal. He is just a man, not God."

Mich looked at me with a frown on his face, and said, "Mom, Johnny is a god to me. He's always been there for me, even when dad wasn't there. He made sure I stayed in school when I wanted to drop out; he told me he wouldn't let me work for him until I finished school. He also told me to go to college, but I had to work for the money. He said he'd only give me one year after I finished high school to work with him to earn enough money to enter college and pay for a full year. After that, he said I would have to get a regular job if my money ran out to pay for the remaining three years of school. He said college would take a lot of work and I needed to concentrate, not sell drugs. He made a deal with me, and he has kept his part of the deal so far. Now, I must be a man and keep my part of the deal. I know you want me to go to college, so I have seven months left before I enroll. I will be going to Georgia University."

I sat completely still, dumbfounded. I couldn't say a word after hearing Mich's story. I wanted to tell Mich everything about Johnny, but how could I do that now? Just then, the waiter came to the table, and we ordered our food. Mich ordered a steak and I ordered a chicken salad. After hearing Mich's story about Johnny, I decided I had to have a drink. I ordered a glass of wine and Mich ordered a fruit drink. The waiter brought our drinks and Mich continued to tell me about Johnny.

"Why didn't you tell me about Johnny before?"

"Johnny told me not to tell you, because you would get mad and not let him do things for me anymore."

"How long have you known Johnny?"

"Since I was a little kid, five or six years old." I gulped my drink down and ordered another one. I took a deep breath. The waiter brought our food and we ate. Mich ate like he had not eaten in a year as he continued to tell me about all the things Johnny did for him growing up. As I ate my food, I started thinking about Johnny. Deep down he must really love me or else he was truly a madman. Or both.

Chapter 17

I picked at my salad while Mich finished his meal and the waiter brought the check. I started to pay the bill when the waiter informed me it had already been paid for.

"By whom?" I asked. He pointed to a table across the room. I turned around and looked in the direction the waiter was pointing and saw Art sitting at a table with two other men having lunch. Mich quickly asked, "Who is that, Mom?"

"No one," I said. "Let's go." I gave Mich the keys to

the car and told him to go on ahead and that I'd be out in a few minutes. Mich hesitated for a moment, but then headed out to the car.

Art stood up as I approached the table.

"I'm surprised to see you here," I said.

"The pleasure is all mine, Peaches," he said. The two guys sharing the table with him got up and went to the bar. Art said, "Please have a seat." I didn't want to, but I did.

"Only for a moment. My son is waiting for me in the car."

Art said, "Oh, so that is your son."

"Yes," I said. "You know, Art, it's strange, but why is it we keep running into each other this way?"

Art moved his shoulders and said, "Maybe it's faith. What do you think, Peaches?"

I didn't answer his crazy talk, but instead asked, "Do you live here, or in New York?"

"I have homes in both cities," he said. I lifted my eyebrow at him, thinking he must be loaded. "Will you have dinner with me tonight?" he asked.

I looked into his eyes with passion and said, "Maybe. Call me on my cell phone tonight around eight." I got up and walked away, leaving Art sitting at the table. I turned around when I got to the door, and Art stood up and gave me a smile. When I got to the car, Mich was standing there waiting.

"What took you so long?" he asked. "I hope you're not friendly with that guy. You know Big J don't take no shit."

I looked at Mich and said, "Get in the car, boy."

In the meantime, Tommy and Rock had found

Danielle and brought her to the house. Johnny was there waiting for them when they arrived. The doorbell rang and Johnny sent the housekeeper to answer the door. She opened the door and told them, "Johnny is waiting for you in the den." They followed her to the den where they found Johnny standing there, smoking a Cuban cigar.

He slowly turned around and said, "Well, well, well, if it ain't Danielle." He motioned to Tommy and Rock and said, "Wait for me in the other room." They left the room without hesitation. Danielle then began to yell profanities at Johnny.

"What do you think you're doing sending those goons to pick me up?" she demanded. "You know I've been working since you kicked me out for that green Jezebel." Johnny got furious at her comment and slapped her as hard as he could.

"Bitch, you don't have to work. I pay you well enough just to keep your damn mouth closed. Furthermore, don't you ever say anything bad about her in my presence. Do you understand?" Danielle stood there looking surprised and holding her face. She looked at Johnny like she couldn't believe he'd just hit her. "Now, that's not why I brought you here. Let's get down to business. Who have you been talking to about me?"

Danielle took her hand off her face and said firmly, "I don't know what you're talking about. Why would I talk to anybody about you?" She moved closer to Johnny and put her hands on his face in a sexual way. He pushed her away and slapped her again. She fell to the floor this time. Danielle looked up at Johnny and said, "I guess the little misses is fulfilling your needs."

Johnny said, "Shut up, Danielle."

She started laughing and said, "What do you want with me, Johnny?"

Johnny went back to the window, picked up his cigar and said, "Someone has been spreading rumors about me and sabotaging my operation. Would you know anything about that, Danielle?"

She sat on the sofa and said, "No! Why should I know anything about that?"

Johnny turned around and looked at her with one eyebrow lifted and said, "You're lying to me, aren't you?"

"No, Johnny, I promise. You know I wouldn't lie about that." Johnny, having been with Danielle as long as he had, knew she was capable of lying, cheating, and stealing if she thought she could get away with it.

With that thought in mind, he walked closer to her, grabbed her neck and said, "You are the only person who has been close enough to me to know about my shipment schedule and Camilla. Not to mention our other little secret."

Gasping for air, Danielle blurted, "Camilla?" Johnny removed his hands from her neck. She said, "What about Camilla?"

"Someone gave Camilla some bogus information about me and set up one of my shipments." Danielle saw the anger in Johnny's eyes and got nervous.

Still standing next to Danielle, Johnny said, "Who have you been seeing?"

"No one," she said.

Johnny pushed her to the floor and said, "You lying bitch. Do you really think I don't know about him?"

Danielle tried to get off the floor, but he pushed her back down. "Who is he?" Johnny demanded. Danielle crawled to the sofa and finally got up. She was terrified at this point. Johnny asked her again. "Who is he, Danielle? I mean business."

"Okay, okay. I just met him and I don't know a lot about him."

"What's his name?" Johnny asked.

In fear of what more Johnny would do to her if she lied, she quickly said, "His name is Art. His name is Art."

"Have you told this Art anything about me?" he asked.

"No, no Johnny. I wouldn't do that; please believe me." Johnny was angry that Danielle would go to another man so soon after him. The thought of her possibly giving information that only she knew made him outraged. Johnny grabbed Danielle's neck and pressed until he heard it pop. He slowly let her lifeless body fall to the floor, then he went to the window, picked up his cigar and lit it. He took a big puff, then put it out. He picked up his cell phone and called Tommy and Rock from the next room. He told them, "Come and get this trash out of my house, right now!" Tommy and Rock rushed in the room and saw Danielle lying there on the floor dead.

"What are you standing there for? Get this trash out!" he yelled. Rock ran toward the door. "Where do you think you're going?"

Rock said, "To get something to put her in."

"Use the rug in here to wrap her up and dispose of the body." Johnny walked out of the room, leaving the two of them to take care of the body. Johnny went to the kitchen and told his housekeeper she could leave for the day, then he went back in the den. Tommy and Rock took the body out to the car, and Johnny gave each of them a one hundred dollar bill and said, "Dinner's on me."

Chapter 18

Sitting in the den all alone, Johnny started wondering who this Art character was and decided he'd better find out and also why he was after him. *Maybe I should not have killed Danielle so quickly. No, no that bitch had to die. There's no telling what she told this man. It's better to have her out of my way for good.* The phone rang. It was Mich calling.

Johnny quickly picked up the phone and said, "Yeah?"

"It's me Big J, Mich. Is it okay for us to come back to the house?"

Johnny said, "I thought I told you to wait until I called you." Mich didn't say anything. Johnny noticed his silence and said, "It's okay, Mich. Come on home." Johnny hung up the phone and said to himself, "Damn that boy has a lot to learn. He's going to get killed, or get his mom or me killed. I need to do something about him quick."

Johnny sat there thinking what to do with Mich. *I know. I'll send his ass off to college now. His mom will be happy, and I won't have to worry about him. I got other things to concentrate on besides him.* Johnny made several phone calls, including one to Georgia University. After he made his last call, he noticed the time. It was now six. *Where the hell is Peaches? It should not be taking them this long to get here. I should never have told her it was okay to get home after dark. Damn!*

Just then the front door opened. Johnny jumped up and went to see who was there. He knew it was Peaches, but he wanted to make sure.

As he walked down the hall to the front door, he heard talking and laugher. It was them. Johnny rushed to Peaches and hugged her tightly.

"What's wrong with you? Did you miss us that much?"

"You know I did. I see you went shopping," he said.

"Yes, Mich needed something to wear besides those jeans and that white T-shirt."

"Okay then. Why don't you go put your bags down and come downstairs? I have something to discuss with you and Mich. Family stuff." I looked at Johnny and thought, *What is he up to now?*

I gave Mich his bags and I ran up the stairs with

mine to quickly put them away. Mich stayed downstairs with Johnny. As I took the items I bought for myself out of the bag, I wondered how things went with Johnny's meeting with Danielle. *And what family stuff does he want to talk about with us? Damn fool acts like we're a real family. Hell, Mich is not his son.* I put on something cozy on and went back downstairs.

Mich was already in the den talking to Johnny when I got there. I entered the room and said, "So, what family stuff do we need to talk about?" I looked at Mich and he had a sad look on his face.

"What's wrong, Mich? Why are you looking like you just lost your best friend?"

"Johnny will tell you," Mich answered. Johnny took over the conversation.

He said, "Peaches, I was just telling Mich since someone is trying to sabotage the operation, I thought it would be a good idea for him to go ahead and enroll in college. That way he will be safe and I won't have to worry so hard about his well being."

I couldn't believe my ears. "Great idea. Johnny is right, baby. This is a dangerous business. You'll be safer at school." *Damn if this ain't perfect!* I said to myself.

Mich looked sadly at Johnny and said, "I guess I won't be getting that ten thousand dollars now."

Johnny said, "As a matter of fact, yes Mich, I'm still going to give you the money. But you have to leave tonight. I've already called the school and arranged everything. So go pack your bags and get ready. The limo will be here to pick you up in half an hour. Hurry, boy."

Mich left the room and went upstairs to pack. Johnny and I stayed in the den. Once Mich was gone out of the room, I looked at Johnny and said, "Thank you," in a soft voice.

He came over to me and kissed my hand. Then he said, "You'll pay me for it, don't worry. Just remember, don't try anything you will regret."

"Johnny, my son is going to college. This is a dream come true. It is something I've always wanted for him. Why would I do something foolish and ruin that?" Johnny got up and went to the window. He got his cigar and lit it.

There was silence in the room, and then I noticed the rug on the floor was gone. "Johnny, what happened to the rug that was on the floor?"

He turned around, looked at me, and said, "I got rid of it."

"Why?" I asked, trying to sound nonchalant.

"It's nothing for you to worry about. We'll get another one—whatever you want." I knew right then and there Danielle would never be seen again. This made me nervous, so I didn't say anything else to Johnny about the rug.

Mich came down the stairs, packed and ready to go. I was so relieved that he was going and getting out of this hell. "Mich, you'll only be an hour away, so don't look so sad."

Johnny looked at Mich and said firmly, "What did I tell you about being a man?"

Mich looked at Johnny and said, "Don't worry, Big J. The next time you see me you'll be proud that I am your..." Then Mich stopped. "You'll see."

The limo arrived and blew the horn.

"Okay Mich, this is it. Give me a hug." I hugged Mich

and gave him a kiss. At the same time I thanked God for getting him away from there. I knew Johnny had just saved his life.

"Okay Big M, I'll see soon." Johnny gave Mich a hug, and Mich left out the door destined for Georgia University.

I turned to Johnny and said, "Could you please order a new rug tomorrow? I don't want anyone to ask you the same question I asked you." I started to walk up the stairs, but then I turned around, looked at Johnny and said, "I have to go out tonight. I'll be back soon. And, don't you start. There is something I need to do. Besides, I don't know why you are worried. Your goons follow me everywhere I go."

Johnny ran up the stairs and grabbed my arms. He turned me around and said, "Where do you think you're going?"

With confidence, I looked him in the eyes and said, "Johnny, what are you afraid of? You have me here with you. You fuck me whenever you want to. You just made me the proudest mom on earth. You could not get rid of me now if you wanted to. The only way you could get rid of me is to kill me." I snatched my arm away from him and continued going to my room. Johnny stood there looking at me. I could feel his eyes stare me down as I walked away. I went in my room and prayed he did not come in. After a couple of minutes had passed, I knew he was not coming to bother me.

I looked in the mirror at myself. *Should I dare go out with Art? Johnny will probably have his goons follow me, so I'll have to lose them.* I went to the closet and decided I'd wear black. I'd never worn black before.

I don't know why. I found a black dress with a low cut back. I knew I couldn't get out of the house showing any tits. I showered, got dressed and found a pair of black heels I bought in New York that went well with the dress. When I looked in the mirror, I saw the most beautiful woman I had ever laid eyes on. *Johnny is going to flip when I go downstairs. He'll know I'm going to see a man. I know just the story to tell.*

I started down the stairs, but then I stopped. I heard Johnny coming. I wanted him to see me at the top of the stairs. He needed to see the Peaches he created. He walked in and looked up at me. I could tell he wanted me right then and there.

He said, "My God, you are beautiful."

I started down the stairs and said casually, "I know." When I reached the bottom of the stairs, I went to Johnny and kissed him softly on his lips and said, "Remember, you created PEACHES." Then I walked away, slamming the door in his face. I looked around outside to see if anyone was there. I didn't see anyone, but that didn't mean anything. Quickly I jumped in the BMW and took off. You could hear the tires burning rubber. I wanted Johnny to hear it too. I couldn't believe I got away with it.

Chapter 19

My date with Art.

I turned the radio on and blasted the Isley Brothers. *That Lady* was playing. I looked down at my purse, got my cell phone out and searched for Art's number. I found the number, dialed it and turned the music back down, not a lot, but just enough so Art could hear it.

Art answered the phone. "Hi Art, this is Peaches. Where do you want me to meet you tonight?"

"Great, Peaches. I see you got away from your man after all."

"Yeah."

"Well, meet me at the 5th Street waterfall. We'll go from there."

"I'll be there in twenty minutes. Looking forward to it," I added. We hung up and I turned the music back up. I was driving and nodding my head to the music when my cell phone rang. I looked at the number and it was Johnny calling me.

Damn, what in the hell does he want? I thought I'd better answer it or he'd keep calling. I turned the music down all the way and answered, "Hello?"

Johnny said, "Peaches, do you want me to wait up for you?" I looked at the phone and chills ran down my spine. It was as if he was there and could see me.

"Yeah, babe. Go get a bottle of my favorite wine—you know the one."

"Sure thing, Peaches." I could hear in his voice he was excited. "By the way, I have something special for you when you get home."

"What?" I asked cautiously.

"You'll see when you get back. Hurry on home."

I hung up the phone. I was not going to let him entice me to come back. I was almost to the waterfall when my cell phone rang again. *Damn this better not be Johnny calling again.* I looked at the phone and it was Art.

Art said, "It's me. Where are you?"

"I'm right around the corner."

"Okay. Just checking."

"I'm five minutes away."

When I got there I saw Art parked in front of the waterfall. I stopped and rolled down my window.

"Hey Peaches, follow me, okay?" He pulled off in his

Mercedes and I followed him. *Damn, I forgot to notice if Johnny's goons were following me. If they do, I'll lie to Johnny the same way he lies to me.* I followed Art for what seemed like miles. *Where the hell is this man taking me?* For a moment my mind flashed a picture of Art attempting to kill me. Not a second later we approached a bar and grill called Club Taz Two Twenty. He pulled in and I parked next to him. I got out of the car and Art walked towards me. He took my hand, kissed it and said, "If you were mine, I would give you the world."

Yeah right. I smiled at him as we walked inside. The club was really nice. The DJ was playing Kenny G's *Silhouette*. That was one of my favorite jazz pieces. Art motioned to someone and a guy came to take us to our table. It was like he had complete control over the place. As we sat down, Art said, "What would you like to drink, Peaches?"

"Red wine, please." I watched Art as he gave the waiter our order. He was dressed very sleek. He had on a grey suit, white shirt, grey tie and black shoes made of the finest leather. I could tell his clothes were tailored. Art checked me out thoroughly as well. I could feel his eyes staring me down in a lustful manner, though he tried to appear like a gentleman.

He started from my head and worked his way down to my toes. The waiter came back with our drinks. "Are you okay? You seem kinda nervous," Art said.

"I'm okay."

"I've been dying for this moment to be alone with you."

"But we're not really alone."

"Well you know, I have a place…"

Damn if I hadn't turned into Katie. Look at me. What the hell was I doing here with this stranger when I had a sick bastard waiting for me at home?

I immediately changed the subject. "Gee, Art, I love this song." The DJ was playing Malo's *Suavecito*.

Art said, "It's one of my favorite songs, too. Would you like to dance?"

"Yes, very much."

As we danced, Art asked, "So Peaches, what would it take for me to take you away from your man?"

"Well it all depends," I answered coyly, thinking about how direct Art was being.

"On what?"

"Well, how do you know I want to be taken?"

"I can see it in your eyes." I looked down. He pulled my chin up with his finger. "Just say the word," he said, kissing me on my lips.

"You don't know what you're getting into."

"Yes, I do, Peaches. I'm getting into you."

I was silent for a while. The DJ started playing Marvin Gaye, *Make Me Wanna Holler*.

Oh now, that's my song. I started to dance separate from Art and he just stood there for a moment watching me. Then he started dancing, following my lead. When the music ended, we went back to our table.

"I love this place, Art. The music's great, the food is delicious, and the company is well, how should I say..." I toyed with him.

"I am glad you like it."

I could tell Art wanted to say something, but was having a hard time trying to get it out. So I changed the subject by asking him, "Why were you in New York?"

"Someone paid me to go there."

"What?"

"Yeah. Just like I said. Someone paid me to go there."

"Well, what do you do for a living?"

"I own a private investigation firm."

Hmm. I was indeed intrigued. "So, you're a PI."

"You could say that, " he answered.

The DJ played Atlantis Starr, *Always*.

"This DJ you have here is great."

"I'll tell him you said so."

I looked at Art and asked, "Do you own this place?"

"As a matter of fact, I do. How did you guess?"

I didn't bother to answer him, since I was keen on watching his lips move as he spoke to me. I was completely mesmerized by the sound of his voice, the music and his manly scent.

"Would you like to dance, madam Peaches?" he said in a seductive tone.

"Yes, oh yes," I replied. We danced very slowly and very close. As I looked into his eyes, I felt magic—an eruption of lust—or was it love?

I could fall in love with this man. Then I thought, *Get a grip on yourself girl.* The music stopped, but we were still dancing.

"The music has stopped, Art."

"I know, baby, but I can do this with you all night."

"Let's go to your place." He did not hesitate. "Okay, let's go." He told the waiter something and then we left. When we got outside, I said, "How far do we have to go?"

"Not far. Do you want to ride with me?"

"Sure." *This way Johnny won't find me,* I figured. I got into his Mercedes. *What a class act,* I said to myself. *This just might be the perfect man for me.* He started the car and we drove off. He put in a CD. It was the Five Stair Steps, *O-O-H Child. How could an Italian know all these good sounds?*

"So tell me Art, how does a man know the right songs to play? You seem to have ESP."

"I owe it all to my sister; she's the music buff. She's the reason I opened the club."

"That's very interesting. Where does your sister live?"

"Italy."

"That seems so far away."

"It is," he said, his eyes looked off into the distance.

"Are you from Italy?" I asked.

"Good guess...yes, I am."

"What about your parents?" I asked.

"Well, my father and mother are deceased. My father's name was Arturo, and my mother's name was Alessandra," he said with a sad look. I did not want to ruin our night, so I let it go.

Art pulled up to a house that made me blink twice.

"Where are we?" I asked.

"We're in Suwannee, Georgia." The house was huge. It looked like a famous person lived there.

"Do you live here alone?" I asked him, trying not to appear overly impressed.

"Yes, except for the help." He parked the car in the garage. He turned the car off and came over to open the door for me. Nice manners.

"Do you want a tour of the house?" he asked.

"It would probably take all night to tour this house!" I smiled.

"Well in that case, we'd better wait until another time," he replied.

As I turned around, Art came up from behind me. At first he scared me, until I realized he was coming after me for something else. Passionately, he started to kiss me. It felt unbelievably good.

But I stopped him.

"Did I do something wrong, Peaches?"

"No, Art. We just have to move slowly, that's all. I like to take my time."

"Well then, would you like something else to drink?"

"Yes, please."

He put on some music...Roberta Flack and Donna Hathaway, *The Closer I Get to You*. Then he brought me a glass of red wine. "How did you know?" I asked.

"Know what?"

"How did you know I wanted red wine? This is my favorite kind."

Gees, he has the exact same kind I'd told Johnny to get for us tonight.

"I just made a good guess," he answered.

"Good guess, all right," I said. I looked deep into Art's eyes, trying desperately to see inside his soul and asked him, "Why are you pursuing me?"

"I thought that's what men did to good-looking women, especially a beautiful woman such as yourself." I took a sip of my wine. He led me to an area of the house that had a plush sofa. The music was playing all throughout the house. We sat down. Then Art looked at me and asked, "Peaches, how do you feel about dating an Italian man?"

"I don't see an Italian man; I see a man. A very attractive, kind and loving man."

"That's all I wanted to know." He put his glass down and started kissing me, gently nudging me backwards so I was lying flat. With great ease, he maneuvered on top of me, kissing my entire body for what seemed like forever. It felt so good that I lost track of time. Then he picked me up and took me to his bedroom. I could not believe my eyes.

Johnny had a big bed, but this man had a really big BED! I thought to myself.

Seductively, he took off my clothes. Then, he started kissing my body slowly and gently. I was writhing in ecstasy. He then penetrated me and it was the most unbelievable climax of my life. I was falling in love with a man I did not know. We made love for what seemed like hours.

When I had a chance to breathe, I looked at the time and saw it was two in the morning. I became frantic.

"I cannot go back to that house tonight."

Art looked at me and asked, "Are you sure?"

"Yes. I want to stay here with you all night." He lay back down and we had sex again and again. It was better than I had ever dreamed. When we finished, we fell asleep in each other's arms.

Chapter 20

I woke up the next morning, happy and with a smile on my face. Then the image of Johnny flickered across my mind. *Damn, Johnny.* I turned on my cell phone and saw that he had called all night. I knew I was in deep trouble. My car was still at the club and if his goons had found it, Johnny would know I was up to no good. *What had I gotten myself into?*

Art entered the room dressed already and smelling good. "You're up early," I said.

"I'm always up early. I brought you something to eat."

"I'm not really hungry," I said. I drank the juice and got in the shower. I stayed in the shower a long time, thinking about our great night of lovemaking and passion, and what I would tell Johnny. *I have some nerve doing this. I'd better come up with something good to tell the bastard or he'll probably kill me!*

As I finished my shower, Art was standing there with a fluffy, snow-white robe. I looked at him and thought — *This has got to be a dream! The man is perfect!*

He wrapped the robe around me. It was warm and soft like nothing I've ever felt. He turned me around, kissed me and said, "I need to talk to you. Please put on your clothes."

He sounded serious, so I figured I'd better hurry and put on my clothes. I didn't want to put the black dress back on, and when I got to the bedroom, Art had some jeans and a shirt for me to wear that was just my size. I got dressed and went into the kitchen where Art was sitting, eating breakfast.

"Have a seat," he said. "You sure you don't want anything?"

"No, Art. I'm fine, but what is it? You're scaring me."

He touched my hand and said, "Don't be afraid. It's nothing bad." He continued eating, saying nothing.

Art finished his meal and wiped his mouth.

"Okay," he said. "Mekia, I know your name is not Peaches."

Right then I stood up and slapped him.

"Sit down for a moment," he said.

"Who are you?" I demanded.

"My name is Arturo. I was sent here to find out

if Johnny is stealing from my sister. I tried to get information from Danielle, but she would not say a word against Johnny."

"So you slept with me and then thought I would tell you what you want to know!"

"No, I slept with you because I fell in love with you the first moment I saw you."

"You liar!!"

"No, it's true," he insisted. "What do you want me to call you? Peaches or Mekia?"

"Peaches," I said.

"Okay. My sister, Camilla, sent me to find out if Johnny was straight."

Camilla is the name Johnny mentioned to Baron and Mich the other day.

"How do I know you are not lying to me?" I asked him.

"Well, you can call my sister and ask her if you'd like."

"So your sister is Camilla, and she has power over Johnny?"

"Well, Johnny actually works for her."

Maybe this is my way out from Johnny!

"Well, what do you want from me, Art?" I asked.

"Have you noticed anything different about Johnny? His behavior, the things he does or anything suspicious lately?"

I thought for a moment and said, "Nothing I can think of. What are you insinuating, Art?"

"Well, Camilla and I think the man you call Johnny is not the real Johnny."

I stood up completely flabbergasted by his statement.

"What the hell are you talking about? You've got to be out of your mind!"

"Sit down, Peaches. I can't talk to you when you're like this." I sat back down. "Camilla has proof from an investigation that we've done, that the man who is calling himself Johnny is not Johnny Robinson."

I could not believe what I was hearing. "It has to be Johnny, because ..." and then I stopped.

"Because what, Peaches?" Art asked. I lowered my head, but could not utter the words. "Are you trying to tell me about the night Johnny tried to rape you twenty years ago and you cut him down the center of his face?" I looked up at him, totally in shock.

"Yes, but how did you know about that?"

"Because my sister took Johnny to a hospital in Italy for surgery on his face."

"So what does that mean?" I asked.

"The man we took to the hospital had plastic surgery and returned to the States. Ten years later, Camilla got word that he was killed, but we could not verify his death. Then Johnny made contact with Camilla. Camilla has not seen Johnny since the surgery."

I put my hands over my mouth in shock. "I don't believe you." Art pulled out a file and opened it. Inside there were pictures of Johnny when he had surgery and pictures of him after surgery. He did not look anything like the man back at the house. There was no scar down the middle of his face. I wanted to cry. "Art ... who is this man I have been living with for the last six months?"

"That is what we want to know," was his reply.

I started to get sick to my stomach. "I have been having sex with this man for nothing. Someone has been playing a game with me."

Art looked at me and said, "Apparently so."

"What do you want from me, Art?"

"We want you to help us find out who this man really is."

"How can I do that?"

"You are on the inside. I can communicate with you and tell you what to look for."

"But he never leaves the house, and he is very suspicious."

"We know. That is why we cannot get close to him. You know Danielle is dead, don't you?" Art said.

I looked at him. "Yes, I figured he killed her. How do you know for sure?"

"Well we followed his goons when they disposed of the body. I'm almost sure Danielle told him about me. So make sure you never say my name."

All this shit was making my head spin. I did not know what to think. "What will you do to him once you find out who he is?"

"We will kill him, of course."

"Wait a minute, Art. My son is involved!! If anything goes wrong, he will surely kill my son."

"We have that under control."

"What do you mean?"

"We've sent Mich to a school in Paris."

I looked at him. "How did you do that?"

"We have ways of doing things," Art said.

"Are you sure Johnny doesn't know where you sent Mich?"

"I'm positive. My connections have never failed," he assured me.

"I hope you're right. When can I talk to Mich?"

"You can call him any time you like. We told him you and Johnny moved to a new house, this house, and gave him this phone number."

I started pacing the floor thinking about Johnny. "What am I going to do now that I have been out all night with you, Art? What will I tell Johnny?"

"I have a plan for that too, so listen closely. I have arranged for your beautiful BMW to be in an accident and you will be in the hospital. I will then have someone make a call to our mysterious Johnny. They will pretend to be the police who are making contact with your next of kin."

I smiled. "That might work," I said.

"I am willing to do anything to finally see this man brought down to his knees! Now Peaches, don't try to be a hero and do something without my instructions, okay?"

"I won't."

"Let's go," Art said. We drove to Northside River Hospital and Art had a room ready for me. There was a fake hospital staff ready to go. Art had a make-up artist come and make my face up with bruises and cuts. Someone made the call to Johnny. I was terrified. I didn't know how I'd be able to continue with the game once I saw the man pretending to be Johnny.

Chapter 21

It was 11:00 a.m. when Johnny arrived at the hospital. I was given a sleeping pill to make me drowsy. Johnny came into the room and held my hand. I opened my eyes slowly. "Peaches, what happened to you? I waited all night for you. I knew something must have happened. I knew you'd never run out on me. I love you so much, baby."

I looked at the man in front of me and tried to figure out who he was. Millions of thoughts scattered through my mind, but nothing clicked. I turned my head and pretended to fall back to sleep. Johnny went out to the nurse's desk and asked what happened. They told him I was in an accident, that a truck hit me and the car flipped over. They told him I was lucky to be alive and that I would need to stay in the hospital a few more days.

"Will she be okay?" he asked, concerned.

"Yes, she has a concussion, but she will be okay," the nurse told him. "We want to monitor her for a few days. She is a very lucky lady." Johnny sat on the bench in the hall with his head in his hands.

Who is this man? I asked myself.

Thirty minutes later, two of Johnny's goons showed up at the hospital. I could hear Johnny fussing at them. "I thought I told you two guys to follow her! What in the hell happened?"

One of the guys said, "We were following her when a car cut in front of us. We lost control of the car and it went down in a ditch. We had to call the tow truck to get us out."

As I listened to their conversation, I figured, Art must have done something, but then the thought faded away.

Johnny continued, "How could you let that shit happen? I pay you to make sure she is okay!"

"What can we do to make it up to you, Johnny?"

"Get out of my face for now!" Johnny walked away from them and came back into my room. He sat in the chair next to my bed. "Peaches, are you awake?" he asked. I was so damned nervous I thought I was in a coma. Finally, being the actress that I am, I turned my head and looked at Johnny with a pitiful look. The make-up artist had done a great job.

"Do you want me to get you out of here?" he asked.

"What did the doctor say?" I asked.

"The doctor said you needed to stay here for a few days."

"Then don't you think we should do what the doctor says?"

With hesitation, Johnny finally said, "Well okay, but they better make sure nothing happens to you while you're here."

"I will be fine. I just need some rest." Then the nurse came in and told Johnny that he would have to leave in five minutes. She was getting ready to give me some pain medicine that would put me to sleep.

He looked at me and said, "I got to go now, Peaches. I will see you in the morning."

"You don't have to come if you have work to do, Johnny. I think I'll be all right in a day or two."

Johnny kissed me on my forehead. "I will be here every day until you come home." He got up and left the room.

Once I knew the coast was clear and Johnny was on the elevator, I sat up in the bed, pulled out my cell phone and called Art. He answered the phone, "Art speaking."

"Johnny just left the hospital. It worked. Where are you?"

"I'm downstairs waiting for a call from my people who are right now at Johnny's house. I'll be up shortly."

"Make sure Johnny doesn't see you."

Art laughed. "So what if he does? He's never seen me before. I'm on my way up."

I sat in the bed holding my knees, rocking back and forth. *How will the game end?*

I had started out on a mission to get Mich away from Johnny, and to make sure he paid for what he had done to my family and me. Now I knew the evil man I feared all my life was dead. My enemy now was a man who actually seemed to love my son and me, and I didn't know why, or even who he was. I sat there and cried until I heard Art enter the room.

"Okay, Peaches, let me give you an update. I had two guys go to the house and search for anything they could find. They found a room behind a mirror on the wall in Johnny's bedroom. Do you know the mirror?"

"Yes."

"Okay. Anyway, the room was filled with pictures of you, your son Mich, your ex-husband, money, and pictures of another woman. I don't know who she is."

"What did she look like?" I asked.

"She had long, black hair—very pretty. The picture had 'love Ruby' on the back of it."

"Yes, yes she was my ex-husband's mother."

"Was she married to Johnny?"

"I don't know. What else was in the room?"

"Well, that is all they told me about. When you called to say Johnny was leaving, I called and told them to get out."

"What will be our next move?" I asked.

"I wish I could take you home with me tonight."

"Why can't you?"

"Well, Johnny may decide to check back up on you later tonight. Remember, he's not a stupid man. And besides, he has very good connections. Just not as good as mine. I have to go now. Try to get some sleep. Remember, Johnny may try to come back later, just to check to make sure the accident was real, so be prepared for him. I will try to come back later if I can. Get some rest." He kissed me and left.

It was around midnight and I was sleeping when I heard someone outside my room. *Who could be here this late? Visiting hours are over.* The nurse had already told me they were gone for the night. I closed my eyes and continued to listen.

Someone entered the room. I stayed still. I could smell a cigar. It was Johnny. I pretended to be asleep, but I could hear him walking back out the door. I opened my eyes and saw him at the door looking at my medical chart. I heard him say, "Let me look at this chart to see if, and where, she's really hurt."

After reading the chart, he shook his head, satisfied. He put the chart down and came back into the room. I kept my eyes closed, pretending to be sleep. I could feel him standing over me. The smell of the cigar was gagging me. He sat down in the chair next to the bed and touched my hand, then picked it up and kissed it. Then he started talking in a low voice.

"I don't know what I would've done if I had lost you, baby. I've got to get you out of this city before you find out. I know you will never forgive me if you find out." He put his head on the bed and started to cry.

I wondered, *Who the hell are you? Please tell me, spill your guts.*

He stayed with me for a while and then abruptly left the room. When I was sure he was gone for good, I got my cell phone and called Art. The phone rang and rang,

Patricia E. Turner

but Art did not answer. I dialed the number again and
he finally answered.

"Art, Johnny was here again. He just left."

"What did he want, Peaches?"

"Just like you said. He wanted to make sure I was
really in an accident."

"Yep. Just like I thought he would."

"And guess what, Art? He almost told me."

"Almost told you what?" Art asked.

"He said he had to get me out of the city before I
found out. He said I would never forgive him if I found
out."

"Is that all he said?" Art asked.

"Yes."

"Okay, then. At least it's a start. He won't be back
tonight, so you should be able to relax now. Our plan is
working."

But I still did not get any sleep that night. The next
morning I wanted to take a shower, but the make-up
artist told me not to. She said she would not be able to
get there until after noon and the make-up would wash
off in water, so I had to take a sponge bath. At 9:00
a.m., Johnny showed up with flowers. They filled up the
whole room.

"Wow, Johnny, you're here awfully early. The flowers
are beautiful."

"Not as beautiful as you are."

"I don't feel so beautiful right now with all these
bruises," I said.

"Nothing could keep you from being beautiful to me,
Peaches." He sat down in the chair next to the bed.

"You know, I came back last night to check on you.

137

You were sound asleep, so I didn't wake you."

"You came all the way back down here last night? How sweet. You know, Johnny, you're a softie. You're not as bad as you try to portray yourself." He just looked at me for a moment without saying anything.

"Well, I'm willing to do, or be, anybody you want me to be. All you have to do is ask."

"I just want you to be who you really are and nobody else," I said, wanting to see how he would react.

He just looked at me strangely and said, "Sometimes you can't be who you really are if you want to survive in this world." He patted me on my shoulder and said, "I got to go now. I'll be back later. But Thursday I won't be here; I have to go out of town."

"Why?" I asked.

"I have to meet a guy who is doing some investigation work for me. He has a report I need to pick up."

"What are you investigating?"

"Danielle gave me some information when we met and I've had someone check it out."

"Danielle? Do you trust her, Johnny?"

"No, but the information she gave may be useful."

"You know, Johnny, I wish I could help you in some way."

"How's that, Peaches? It's a tough killing world out there."

"Well, just like now, maybe I might be able to help you figure out something regarding what Danielle told you."

"I doubt it."

"Come on, Johnny, what could it hurt? You do trust me, don't you?"

"Yes, Peaches."

"Then let me help you. You have to trust somebody besides all your goons." He looked me straight in the eye. "I had to trust you when I moved in with you, right? You kept your promise not to hurt Mich."

"I was never going to hurt Mich," he said. "I wanted you."

"Well, you have me now, don't you?" He didn't say anything.

"Johnny, I know you killed Danielle." His eyes pierced mine. "And I haven't gone to the police," I said. "That should tell you something about my trust and loyalty."

"Danielle was a problem. I got rid of her so we could be together. Then I found out she was giving information to some new guy she was dating named Art." Just then the nurse came into the room. *Perfect timing, Ms. Fake Nurse.*

"Ms. Robinson, it's time to take your medication," she interrupted.

Johnny got up and said, "I gotta go, Peaches. I'll see you later."

"But Johnny, what about our conversation?"

"What conversation?" he acted like he'd forgotten what I'd just said. "You need to focus on getting well," he said, and abruptly left the room. I pulled out my cell phone and called Art. The phone rang and he answered.

"Art, it's Peaches. I've got some big news. Johnny was just here. He told me he's leaving town tomorrow to meet with an investigator. He said he hired someone to find out about a man named Art. This means trouble."

"Don't worry, Peaches. He won't find anything on me.

Only you and Danielle know me as Art, and Danielle is dead. I gave myself that nickname when I took this case. Don't worry about what your boy Johnny said."

"Okay, you're the boss."

"Hey Peaches, how about if a new doctor comes in and examines you later today?" he giggled. I had to think about what he was saying.

"Who, you?"

"Who else?"

"Stop being fresh and bring your tools with you."

He laughed and said, "No doubt. See you later."

"Wait a minute! What if Johnny comes back later?"

"Don't worry, he won't."

Around one, Johnny called and said he wouldn't be able to make it back to the hospital. I acted like I was really disappointed. "I won't see you until Friday when I get back into town, but I'll get you something to make up for not being there."

"Okay, babe, I'll miss you. Hurry home." I hung up the phone, rolling my eyes. I was not interested in anything he could bring me. I was already past his dick; I was thinking about Art and tonight.

Later on around eight, Art arrived at the hospital with more flowers and chocolates. He walked in dressed sleek as usual and smelling oh so good. I couldn't get his scent out of my mind. His cologne must have been very expensive. He gave me the chocolate and kissed me on the lips. "How is the patient tonight?" he asked.

"I don't know, Doc. I have a pain you may need to check out."

"Oh yeah, where is this pain?" he said in his sexy accent.

"It's right here," I said while pointing to my private area.

"I tell you what, Miss. You may need some surgery, so let me take you to the operating room." He kissed me long and hard. Then he said, "Let's go. I've arranged for you to leave the hospital and return in the morning."

"But ..."

He put his hands over my mouth and said, "Don't worry about your boy, Johnny. I got that covered." I put on my clothes and we left the hospital. We hugged as we walked to Art's car. Suddenly out of the corner of my eye I saw two guys sitting and watching us from a black Monte Carlo.

"Art, look, those two guys work for Johnny."

"Stay calm. There's nothing to worry about. Get in the car." He closed the door and pulled out his cell phone. I couldn't hear what he said, but I knew it had something to do with the two guys in the car. Art got into the car.

"What are we going to do now? They'll tell Johnny!" Tears came to my eyes.

Art looked at me and said, "Peaches, they won't tell Johnny. You've got to trust me." He held me and rubbed the back of my head, then looked at me and said, "We don't know who this man is right now. Until I find out, you don't have to worry about him harming you. Trust me, you'll see."

He cranked up the car, turned on the music, and slowly pulled off. He drove like he wanted the two guys to see us. I closed my eyes and looked away. As we drove away, they followed. Art looked in the mirror, but did not say anything. We stopped to pay the parking attendant, and then Art slowly drove off, waiting for the two bullies. As we drove, I noticed Art was not going in the same direction we had gone to his house the last time.

"I thought we were going to your place."

"We are. I'm taking the long way until our two friends are no longer following us." Art drove to a dirt road. I had no idea where we were. He slowed down because there was a parked car in front of us. Art drove by the car and stopped. The two guys following us continued on their mission. I looked in the rearview mirror to find the parked car we had just passed now following the two guys. Art sped up and suddenly I saw a big explosion. Art looked at me and said, "I told you they wouldn't tell Johnny. My people never fail me."

Chapter 22

When we arrived at Art's house, I was so shaken up I did not pay attention to the time. He parked in the garage, got out and headed inside. *Did he forget about me?* No sooner did the thought cross my mind, than he came back to the car, opened the door, picked me up, and carried me inside. He did not put me down until we reached the bedroom. He put me on the bed and then filled my mouth with white wine and his kisses.

"Can I take a quick shower?" I asked.

"Later, Peaches. You smell like something sweet to me right now." With that he ripped my clothes off with passion and began to sex me in ways I've never known. I woke up the next morning in a daze, trying to figure out where I was. Art appeared at the bedroom door with a tray of food. I thought about Johnny, but the thought quickly left my mind. He had fruit, juice, coffee, and pancakes with whipped cream.

"This looks great!" I was starving. I ate everything on the tray, then got up and went to take a shower. The water felt great. I had not had a good shower since we faked the accident. When I finished showering, Art had the white robe waiting for me. He had also bought me underwear and new clothes. What a thoughtful hunk of a man. "Thank you, Art. You're so thoughtful and know my taste perfectly."

He looked at me and said, "You are most welcome, Peaches." I felt so good.

Art said, "Before I take you back to the hospital, we need to talk. Hurry and get your clothes on. I'll be waiting downstairs for you." He left the room and I put on my clothes. When I got downstairs, Art was sitting in the kitchen drinking coffee.

"May I have some more of that?" I asked politely.

"What? The coffee or me?"

"I can't handle any more of you right now. Just let me have the coffee."

"All jokes aside, Peaches, have a seat."

As I sat down with my cup of coffee, Art said, "I found out something about your mysterious Johnny."

Excitedly I asked, "What is it?"

"Johnny didn't have all the books to show Camilla. He

told Camilla someone destroyed part of the information, and he thought it was Danielle. Camilla has no time for his cowardice and lies. She wants Johnny dead. No time for any games. I pleaded with Camilla not to do anything just yet. Not until we can find out his true identity. I asked her to let me do what I do best. If we kill him now, we may never know who he really is."

"Thank you, Art. I really appreciate that. I must know who he is." We finished our coffee and he took me back to the hospital.

"Just know, Peaches, the countdown on Johnny's life is on ..."

I got back to the hospital room. The make-up artist fixed my face back so it looked slightly bruised, as if I was beginning to heal. When she finished, she said good-bye and I turned on the TV. The news was on, and I turned the volume up. There was a report about a black Monte Carlo with two men that had exploded, killing them instantly. The police had no information on what caused the accident. I turned the TV off.

Your new man, Art, killed those two guys. What did I expect? The man was part of a drug cartel. Hell, Johnny would have done the same thing. For some reason, I felt a little sick to my stomach, I just put it off as exhaustion from playing with Art all night. I lay down and fell asleep. When I woke up, it was Thursday morning. Art called to say he would be out of town and would not return until Friday.

"I'll see you when you return. Be safe." Then I hung up the phone. I could tell he wanted to tease me about the night before, but I didn't want to give him the satisfaction of bragging. For some reason, I still didn't feel very well. It must have been the wine. I can't drink white wine. Art would have some news about Johnny when he returned. I couldn't wait.

I started to think about Mich and how much I missed him. I knew I shouldn't call him, because I would have too much explaining to do. Then I decided, what the hell. I needed to talk to my son. I got my purse and found the phone number Art had given me. I dialed the number and Mich answered the phone. I was so excited to hear his voice.

"Mich, are you okay?"

"Yes, Mom. I'm great. I love it here. I've met a lot of new friends, and there is so much to see and do here."

"I'm so happy to hear your voice, Mich, and I'm so glad things are going well."

"How are you and Johnny doing, Mom?" I hear you guys moved into a new house."

"Yes we did, and I love it, baby. I can't wait to see you. Maybe we can come to visit you soon."

"That sounds good Mom, but I've been so busy."

"I bet you have. College is different from high school, isn't it?"

"Yes, but I met someone Mom."

"Oh yeah? Who?"

"I met a girl named Marie," he said. Then someone started talking to Mich in the background. He finally came back to our conversation and said, "Mom, I got to go now. I'll try to call you some other time."

"Okay, Mich. Love you."

"I love you too, Mom. Bye." I sat there holding the phone, thinking, *My son is turning into a young man. He probably won't be calling me anytime soon. He is falling in love.* I hung up the phone and sat there in a daze. I finally got my mind off him by flipping through some books that were lying on the table. One cover got my attention. It was a book published by 5ᵗʰ Street Books entitled, *Who Can You Trust?*

That sounded interesting. I started reading the book and could not stop. I read the whole book and then fell fast asleep.

It was the middle of the night when I heard voices outside my room. I opened my eyes, but did not see anyone there. As I started to turn over to go back to sleep, a woman appeared in the doorway. She was dressed in a dark-colored suit with a hat, and she wore white gloves. There were two big guys wearing suits and dark shades standing behind her. I sat up in the bed, pulling the covers up to my neck and asked, "Who are you?"

The woman came close to the bed, turned on the light and said, "So, you are the woman who has Arturo's mind occupied."

I didn't know what to think, so I said again, "Who are you?"

She said, "I am Camilla, Arturo's sister."

I wanted to say, *"It's nice to meet you,"* but I didn't think she wanted to hear that.

Instead she blurted, "You're black."

"Yes, ma'am," I said, thinking, *No shit.*

"Let me make something crystal clear to you, young lady. You may be dating Arturo, but do not think for a second that he will marry you. My family does not cross racial lines or mix racial blood, especially black blood. Have your fun if you must, but keep in mind, I will not allow you to marry him. In case you are interested, you are not the kind of woman Arturo would bring to see his family or me. If you are smart, you will not see him again."

One of the guys with her took her hand and led her out of the room. I sat there in shock. I didn't know what to do or think. What a woman. She was definitely not the kind of woman you wanted to mess with.

I wondered what Art would say when I told him. Should I even tell him she came to see me? I pulled out my cell phone to call Art, but I could not dial the number. I threw the phone on the bed and lay back on the pillow. *Art and I make a perfect couple. I love him. How can she ask me to give him up?* I thought.

Chapter 23

It was 8:00 a.m. and the sun was shining. A normal person would be getting ready to enjoy the beautiful day. But me, I was not a normal person these days. I was a woman being tormented by a man I didn't even know. To add insult to injury, I had a vicious woman trying to decide the outcome of my future with the man I loved. The more I thought about it, the angrier I got. I was packing my stuff when Johnny showed up. He stuck his head inside the door with flowers covering his face. *Damn, here I go with this stupid game.*

"Did you miss me?" Johnny asked playfully.

I turned around to continue packing. He grabbed me around the waist and kissed me on the neck. I looked down at his hand and saw he had a bandage on it.

"What happened to your hand?"

"Oh, that. I ran into some trouble."

"What kinda trouble?" I asked.

"Some guys, probably the same person who is trying to sabotage me, attacked me."

"Where were your people?" I asked.

"They showed up late."

"Did you see the news? Tommy and Rock got killed in a car explosion the same day."

"I don't know what's going on, Peaches."

"Well, did you find out anything about this Art character that Danielle told you about?"

"No, I ran into a dead-end with the investigation. It's strange. The investigator, Chuck, could not find anything on the guy. He thinks he may be using a fake name."

"Damn, that's too bad."

Johnny picked me up, swung me around, and said, "So, are you ready to go home?"

"Yes! I can't wait to get home!" Then I asked, "What about my car? I forgot to ask you about it."

"It's in the shop," he said. "It will be ready later today. I will send someone to pick it up for you."

"How bad was it? The car, I mean?" I said.

Johnny said, "Well, it was bad, but not totaled. The important thing is, you are all right."

The fake nurse came in, packed my flowers, and pushed me out to the car in a wheelchair. Johnny questioned the second set of flowers. I told him they came from people at my old job and he let it go.

We arrived at Johnny's house at 9:30 a.m. Johnny helped me into the house.

"What do you want me to do with all these flowers?" he asked.

"Put them on the patio. I'll deal with them later." I started up the stairs as Johnny came back inside.

He looked at me and yelled, "Stop!"

"What?" I asked, somewhat scared, somewhat surprised.

"I can't let you walk up those stairs." He came up to me, picked me up and carried me to my room. He sat me on the bed, kissed my forehead and said, "Whatever you need to get better, I am here."

"I'm fine, Johnny, really. I just need to get my strength back. A little more rest ought to do it."

"Okay, then let me go bring the rest of the flowers to the patio." He left the room and I sighed. *I need to find out who he is. I don't know if I can wait until Art returns. Maybe I just should ask him, just outright ask him who he is.* For some strange reason, I started to feel pity for him. I was thinking about what Art said about killing him.

I took a shower and laid across the bed, thinking about the night Camilla came to visit me. *Maybe I should ask Johnny about her. Maybe I can say Mich told me about her and see what Johnny says. Yes, that's what I'll do.* Just as I started to head downstairs, Johnny opened the door.

"You startled me, Johnny."

"Where are you going?"

"I was coming to see what you were doing," I smiled at him coyly.

"I was making some calls. What do you need?"

"Well, Johnny, I wanted to talk to you about something."

"Okay, what is it?"

"Mich mentioned something about the vicious woman named Camilla that you work for."

Johnny said, "Why did Mich say anything to you about her? That is why I had to send him away from here. He was bound to get someone hurt or killed."

I looked at him and said, "Is that why you sent him away?"

Johnny said, "Yes, to protect him." I settled back down once I heard that.

"But Johnny, who is this Camilla woman?"

"She is a man you never want any ties to."

"Johnny, you called her a man."

"Yes, I know, because she has a heart of stone. I'm surprised she has not killed me."

"What do you mean, Johnny?"

"Well Peaches, you see, someone stole part of my books. I was not able to show her what she wanted. Any other person would be dead by now, but for some reason, she gave me a second chance. I guess I'm either a lucky man or a man walking on thin ice. Which brings me to a point to ask you a question. Would you be willing to leave Atlanta with me?"

"What? I can't leave here. I have my house and ... no, Johnny. Why do you want to leave Atlanta?"

"If I don't leave, it's just a matter of time before Camilla will have me killed."

"But I thought you said she gave you a second chance."

"Do you really think I believe she is not going to kill me? I'm not a stupid man. I don't know why she gave me a second chance, but I do know I'm a walking dead man."

I looked at him and felt sorry for him. *What a stupid fool I have become. In love with Art and still a sucker for Johnny, aka, who knows who.*

"Johnny, come here and sit next to me." He came over and sat on the bed. I looked him straight in the eyes and asked him, "Johnny, is there something you want to tell me?"

The room was silent. We were looking directly at one another. His eyes were familiar, yet different. I couldn't place what it was, but something was definitely different.

"Yes, but now is not the time."

He got up and started for the door as I called out after him, "Wait!" He turned around and faced me. "I know you are not Johnny."

He stood there staring at me for a long moment and then said, "What do you mean?"

"You're not who you say you are. You're not Johnny Robinson, are you?"

"Then who am I, Peaches?" He turned and left the room. It was the million-dollar question.

I sat there on the bed, analyzing what had just happened.

It wasn't my imagination—he had just admitted to me he was not Johnny. I needed to think. I needed to get out of the house. I was nervous about what had just happened. Where the hell was Art when I needed him? Then I thought about Camilla's mean-spirited comments at the hospital.

Will Art let her interfere with our relationship, or will he stand up for me? Can I trust Art to help me get away from Johnny?

I had to trust him. I have to finish the game. In the meantime, I will just deal with the shit. To take my mind off this confusion, I started listening to my stomach rumble. I hadn't eaten for a day, but I didn't dare ask Johnny for anything.

An hour passed, and I decided to fight the hunger pangs and took a nap. All this mind game playing was making me tired. I fell asleep quickly. Later on, I opened my eyes and saw the sun was going down. I jumped up to look at the clock and realized it was 7:45 p.m. I went out in the hallway, looked over the balcony, and saw no sign of Johnny. I decided to go downstairs and search the house. I looked in every room, but he was not there.

Where could he be? I went to the garage to see if the BMW was there and it was. I was happy to see my car. I noticed Johnny's truck was not here, so I went back into the house, got my keys and purse, and left. My first stop was Mac 5th to get a salad. I parked and ate in the car. I pulled out my cell phone to call Art.

"Hey Art, it's Peaches. What time will you be back?"

"Early."

"Good, I will be waiting on you."

"Do you miss me?" he asked.

"That depends on how you answer some questions I have for you."

"About what?" he asked.

"It's something I need to discuss with you in person."

"Okay, Peaches. No problem. I've got to admit, you're making me very curious about what you want to discuss."

"I don't mean to. I just want to be able to see your face when we talk."

"Well, I have something for you as well. Some new information on your boy Johnny."

"You do? What? What?" I asked.

"No way! I'm not going to give this information up until I get back."

"I guess we both have something to look forward to. I'll see soon."

I hung up the phone, left Mac 5th and went back to the house. When I got there, Johnny was back. I parked and went inside the house.

"Johnny! Johnny! Hello?" I called. There was no answer. I went into the den and found Johnny sitting in his chair, smoking his cigar.

"Have a seat." He was looking at me, puffing on his cigar. "Well, what do you want to know, Peaches?"

"I want to know who you really are."

"What makes you think I'm not Johnny? It's hard for me to believe you analyzed all this and have suddenly determined I'm not who I am. What's going on, Peaches?"

"Don't try to turn this around. I bet you can't look me in the eyes and say you are Johnny Robinson. The real Johnny would not hesitate to set the record straight, but you can't do that."

He went to the window, still puffing his cigar, turned back around to face me, and said, "Peaches, I'm not buying this bullshit you are trying to pull." He sat back down and said, "Who is he?"

My heart pounded and I could not speak. I sat there for a moment in silence, trying to quiet my spinning head. *He is fishing for answers; he doesn't know a thing.* I got up, walked over to him and slapped him as hard as I could, then walked away. When I got into the hall, I ran up the stairs to my room, locked the door and leaned up against it. I was hoping he wouldn't come up behind me, because I was fresh out of bright ideas. *What just came over me? I can't believe I slapped him.* I smiled and went to sit next to the window. *He can't possibly know anything about Art. I know he is just fishing for information. Art has never left any loose ends, and I'm going to play my cards on that. Johnny will have to come to me and apologize for insinuating I am involved with someone. He has no proof, and I am not telling. Let him make the next move.*

I was glad I had gone to get something to eat earlier. I changed my clothes and got into bed. I was not sleepy. I just lay there waiting for Johnny to make his move. He had no choice but to come to me and apologize.

I got up and found my photo album. I looked at pictures of the many stages in my life, like Katie, Aunt Maggie, me in high school, Don, Mich's baby pictures, and other special moments. For some reason, I was drawn to pictures of Don and how much we loved each other. He was such a handsome man. Then I heard the knock on the door. I got up and went to answer it. In an angry voice, I said, "What do you want?"

"Will you please open the door?" he begged. By the tone of his voice I thought, *I got him.* I opened the door and saw him standing there with two glasses and a bottle of wine.

I turned, walked away and sat back on the bed as he entered the room and closed the door.

He said, "I want to apologize. I had no reason to say those things to you. I have your favorite wine chilled just the way you like it as a peace offering." He poured me a glass and then poured himself one. He sat beside me on the bed. "Can you forgive me, Peaches?" I told myself, *"Remember, you must finish the game."*

"Yes, I guess so," I told him, my voice devoid of emotion.

"Great!" he said excitedly. "I sure did miss you these last couple of days."

"I missed you too," I said. He kissed me on the lips, then put his glass down on the nightstand. He took mine too, as he leaned me back and started kissing and playing with me. He was driving me crazy with anticipation. The sex was quick; he must have had something on his mind.

Afterwards, I carefully broached the subject once again. "You still owe me an answer to my question." He looked at me with sadness in his eyes and said, "You already know the answer. Think about it."

He got up and put his clothes on. He walked towards the door, turned around and said, "As many times as we've had sex, I can't believe you don't know. Did you ever really love me?" He left the room, slamming the door. I heard him leave the house. I went to the window and saw him pulling away in his truck. I sat in the window with a blanket over me.

Over and over in my mind, I heard his voice saying, *"Did you ever love me?"* I paced the floor all night, but Johnny did not come back to the house.

The next morning when I got up, Johnny still was not back. I took a shower and put on a black pantsuit with heels. I looked in the mirror and decided I needed to go to the salon. The make-up was finally gone from the fake accident, and I was ready to look good again. I couldn't sit there in that house worrying about my mystery man. He'd come back.

I got to the salon and Drew was waiting for me. He talked about his usual guy stuff and I just listened. I didn't do much talking because I was too busy thinking about what Johnny had said to me, *"Did you ever love me?"*

Before I knew it, Drew was finished with my hair. I got into my car and turned on the music; Atlantic Starr's *Always and Forever* was playing. It made me cry. I went back to the house, but he still was not back yet and it was after six. I did not go inside. Instead I drove around.

While driving, I heard my cell phone beep. When I checked it, Art had called me four times. "Damn! I have to call him back," I said aloud.

I dialed his number and he answered.

"It's me, Peaches."

"I thought you were anxious to talk to me."

"I am."

"Where are you?" he asked.

"I'm just driving around," I answered.

"Can you find your way back to my house?"

"Sure. I'll be there in forty minutes. See you soon."

I drove at the speed limit and I did not care if anyone was following me. Art's guys were bigger and badder than Johnny's. I had nothing to be afraid of any more.

I wonder what information Art has that will prove who Johnny is. I was anxious to know the truth. Soon the game would be over and I could go back to being normal again. If Art refused to stand up with me against Camilla, it wouldn't matter. I would still have the one thing that mattered to me most, and that was Mich.

I finally arrived at Art's house. Before I could ring the doorbell, Art opened the door. I could hear music playing throughout the house and it sounded lovely. Art greeted me with a kiss on the lips and invited me inside. I was so happy to see him. He looked great and smelled good, too. I sat down on the sofa and he asked me if I wanted something to drink. I needed something stronger than wine. "A martini, please."

He looked at me strangely and said, "You must be uptight. Let me try to help you relax." He fixed the drink and brought it to me. Then he went back to the bar and got himself a drink. He came back and sat beside me. "Now, tell me what's going on."

I looked at him, thinking how much I loved him. "Art, do you love me?" I asked.

"You know I love you," he said.

"No, Art. I don't know. We have not been together that long. We really don't know each other, do we?"

"What are you talking about?" he asked, his eyes searching mine.

"Camilla came to visit me while I was in the hospital."

Art stood up. "Why didn't you tell me? She had no right to do that!" Immediately he went to the telephone and picked it up.

"No! Art don't call her! Let me finish." He put the

phone down and sat back down next to me. "Camilla told me some disturbing things."

"What did she say to you?"

"Well, she told me that she would never allow you to marry me and that your family never mixed blood. Is that true, Art?"

He looked at me strangely. "That is Camilla talking. She has this mixed-up thing in her mind that she will find me the perfect woman to marry. She is obsessed with making sure I marry and have the perfect daughter, since she's never been able to have a child. Camilla is the only girl in the family in twenty years. My other two brothers all had boys. Her brothers all had boys. I guess she thinks I am the chosen one in the family to have this perfect daughter. But what she doesn't realize is that I will make the choice as to whom I will marry. And that woman will be you."

As I hugged him tightly, a tear fell on his shoulder. "There is no reason for you to cry, my sweet Peaches. You should be happy, because you will be Mrs. Arturo Battista." He pulled a box out of his pocket and opened it. It was the biggest diamond ring I had ever seen.

He put it on my finger, kissed me and asked, "Will you give me the honor of being my wife?"

"Yes, yes, yes. I will!" I shouted in jubilee. We kissed and hugged, but then I pulled away. "What will you tell Camilla about us?"

"I'll tell her that you are going to be part of our family."

"Are you sure?" I asked.

"Yes, I'm positive. You'll see. It will be all right." I was happy about him asking me to marry him, but deep down I still knew in my gut that Camilla would never accept me. There was going to be trouble. I vividly remembered the night she came to the hospital. She was serious about what she had told me and this frightened me a lot. Art stood up and asked, "Will you dance with me?"

"Anything you want from me is yours."

"I hope you mean that," he said.

We danced and kissed, and smiled, and admired my beautiful diamond ring.

Art interrupted my daydream of our wedding day. "Baby, I need to tell you something."

I was so happy, I'd forgotten all about Johnny.

"Yes, Art?" I said with my head lying on his chest.

"We need to talk about your boy Johnny."

"Yes. Yes. Please tell me everything you found out, Art."

"You better sit down for this one, Peaches. I had some more research done on Johnny, and this is what I found. Are you ready?"

"I am as ready as ever to get him out of my life. I need to hear the truth."

Art began slowly, "Camilla had arranged for Johnny to pick up a large shipment, and Johnny took his son with him."

"Who? Don?"

Art took a deep breath and said, "Yes, Don. They had to go into Mexico and while they were there, they got ambushed by a group of thugs. Johnny got killed during a fight with one of them. He was stabbed to death with a knife, but Don managed to escape. He got help from some of the Mexicans by promising them something. He made contact with Camilla pretending to be Johnny and told her what had happened. Camilla arranged for a rescue team to come and get him and the shipment. When they got there, things got out of hand and another fight broke out. They managed to get to the plane, but the plane crashed. When Camilla's crew found the plane, Don had injuries all over his face. He was taken to a hospital and they suggested plastic surgery, but he refused and left the hospital.

From that point on, Don came back to Atlanta and started pretending to be Johnny. It has worked so far. I don't have any other details about how he made himself look so much like Johnny, though. I did find one report stating that Don did eventually have surgery on his face."

I sat in silence, completely stunned. Art left me alone. He knew there was nothing he could do to stop my pain. I went to the bar and downed a few shots of vodka to numb the pain.

"What is Camilla going to do about him now?" I asked.

"She is waiting on me to let her know when to go."

"Go? What does that mean, Art?"

"I told you, Peaches. She put off killing him until I finished this investigation. I did that because you wanted to know who he was. I did this all for you, Peaches."

"Can you please hold off Camilla a little longer? Please?"

"How long do you need? And why?"

"Can you give me a few weeks?"

He looked at me with bewilderment in his eyes. "A few weeks? I don't know about that. Why Peaches? I thought you hated this man and couldn't wait to see him dead."

"Please, Art? There is something I need to do."

"I will hold her off as long as I can."

"Thank you," I said. "Will you please contact an attorney tomorrow so I can have him start preparing to file divorce papers for me?"

"Yes, I will do that for you," he said.

I made up a fake excuse to get out of there. I had to see Don and set the record straight. I couldn't believe it was really him all along.

Kissing Art, I whispered in his ear, "I'll be back for you later, my love."

As I was driving back to the house, my mind swirled with disturbing thoughts. *What was Don thinking, doing something so stupid? I will never forgive him for what he has done to Mich and me. I can't wait to hear what he has to say!* I was driving a bit over the speed limit and was rather tipsy from the drink I just had, so I decided to slow down. Turning on the radio, I looked up to find a car heading straight toward me. I jerked the car in a panic and lost control. The last thing I remember was screaming Art's name.

Chapter 24

Now what?

I opened my eyes and all I could see were lights beaming down on my face. "Where am I?" I shouted.

A nurse appeared and said, "Calm down. You're okay. You were in a terrible accident." I tried to sit up, but I got dizzy.

The nurse said, "Please Miss, lay back down. You have been in a coma for six weeks. You are lucky to be alive."

"Six weeks?" "Has anybody been here to see me?" I asked.

"Yes, your husband, Mr. Robinson." The nurse went to the window and opened the curtains. She turned around and said, "Your husband was very worried about you and the baby."

My eyes got big. "What baby?"

"You are three months pregnant. You didn't know?"

Suddenly I got sick and started to vomit. The nurse got the bedpan and asked, "Are you okay? Do you need something to drink?"

"No, thank you." I felt my stomach and there was a little pouch.

I started thinking about what had happened and remembered I was at Art's house, and he had asked me to marry him. I looked at my finger, but the ring was not there. I asked the nurse, "Did you take my jewelry?"

"Yes, we locked your ring and earrings away."

I sighed. "How long am I going to be in here?"

"Well, we were waiting for you to come out of the coma. The baby will be fine. We have been feeding you two intravenously. The doctor will want to run a few more tests before he releases you. Are you hungry?"

"Yes, very. What time is it, and what day is it?"

"It's Wednesday, August 5th, and it's 6:00 p.m. Your husband gets here faithfully every day at 6:15 to sit with you. He should be here in fifteen minutes. Would you like a mirror to brush your hair?"

"Yes, please." When I looked in the mirror, I saw deep scars on my face from the accident. There was one over my eye and one on my chin. *Who did this to me?*

Then I remembered someone had tried to kill me. I

got really nervous and afraid for my baby. I was in a panic. *Whose baby is this anyway? Art's or Don's? What a mess I have gotten myself into!* It was 6:15 p.m. on the dot, and as I turned to the door, the man I used to love was standing in there. He was no longer disguised as Johnny. He had a small scar on his face just under his eye. He was not wearing black; he had on some jeans, a blue shirt, and a cap.

He came to me and hugged me, then kissed my forehead. "Mekia, I am so sorry for all the pain I have caused you. Please don't ask me why I did such a stupid thing, because all I would be able to tell you is that I thought I was doing the right thing for us at the time. I knew you would not come back to me if I tried to explain to you what Johnny made me do. I tried several times to tell you the truth, but something always stopped me. He was a bad man, Mekia, and he had a way of getting people to do things. I got him killed when we were in Mexico. I knew I had to get rid of him for Mich and your safety. If you can't find it in your heart to forgive me, just tell me that you understand why I did it."

"Don believe it or not, I do understand why you had him killed. But I will never understand why you took me through such torment. You could have told me the truth. I spent my whole life waiting for someone like you to come along. I didn't have sex for years because all I thought about was you."

He smiled. "Well all those years were worth the wait! You are awesome in bed." I hit him on his head and we laughed.

"Get up! I am serious Don. You don't know how

much shit I have gotten myself into thinking you were Johnny."

"Do you think we can still live together for the baby's sake?"

I looked at him with my mouth open. "This is not your baby."

"What do you mean, it's not my baby?"

"I have been seeing someone else for four months."

He looked at me with regret in his eyes. "Who is he?"

"You don't need to know that."

"How do you know it's not my baby?"

He's right; I don't know for sure. Then I said, "I just know."

"You can't just say you know who the father is when you have been sleeping with two men. You need to make sure who the father of this child is. I have a right to know. Let's have a test before you leave the hospital." Angry with him for thinking he was the father, I agreed.

Don went to get the doctor and brought him back to the room. The doctor looked at me and asked, "Mrs. Robinson, are you sure you want to have this test?"

"Yes, I'm sure."

They had the nurse prepare me for testing. The results would be back the next day. They took a blood sample from Don, and he told me he would be back in the morning. "Mekia, if the baby turns out to be mine, will you think about staying with me?"

I turned my head and did not answer him. *If this baby is his, I am going to kill myself. There is no way I would have another baby for someone who tortured me the way he did. I don't care what his reasons were.* Then

I started to think about Art. I wondered if he had been to the hospital and if he knew about the baby. After the test was taken, I was emotionally drained and fell right to sleep.

Around eight, I awoke from someone kissing me on my cheek. It was Art. I was so glad to see him! "Where have you been?"

"I've been here every night since the accident."

"How did you know I was in an accident?"

"It was all over the news. The driver of the car that ran into you was killed instantly." He held his head down.

"What's wrong, Art?" I asked.

He was silent for a moment, and then he said, "I am worried because I think the driver was one of Camilla's goons."

"What?"

"Yes, I think Camilla tried to have you killed." I hugged him and began to cry.

"Do you know about the baby?" I asked.

He pulled away from me. "The baby?"

"Yes, the baby. I just found out when I came out of the coma. The nurse told me I am three months pregnant. Art, I just know it's your baby."

"How do you know it's my baby?"

"It's yours. I just took a test tonight to prove it because Don, aka Johnny, wanted to know if he is the father or not. He also told me all about what happened with him and Johnny in Mexico. He refuses to believe this baby is not his, but I know it's your baby. We will know for sure tomorrow."

"If you know in your heart that this baby is ours,

then I believe you." He kissed me again and said, "I have to go. I need to talk to Camilla and set things straight. I did not want to confront her until I knew you would be all right. Now that you are okay, and I know I am going to be a father, I need to talk to her immediately." Art left the hospital, happy he was going to be a father.

Chapter 25

Who's the father?

Morning came quickly; I woke up feeling like a mother-to-be. I had morning sickness. I slept well last night. *It must be because the baby was pleased that she had some real food.* I was anxious to get the test results back.

I had no taste for the hospital food, so I called Art to ask him to bring me some real food. He asked when he should come.

"I want you to come now."

"What about Don?"

"I don't care if Don sees you. You are the father of my child and my future husband."

"I am on my way."

I wonder what happened when he talked to Camilla? I guess he will tell me when he gets here.

The nurse came into the room and announced, "Mrs. Robinson, we have the test results back. Would you like to wait, or do you want me to tell you now?"

"Please tell me now," I insisted.

"The test results reveal that Don Robinson, Jr. cannot be the father of this child."

"Thank you, God!"

"Mrs. Robinson, we also have the sex of the baby, if you want to know."

"It's a girl, isn't it?"

The nurse said, "Yes, how did you know?"

"I just knew." *This time I am going to make sure this marriage works. This baby girl will not grow up without her father like I did.* I rubbed my stomach and said softly, "I promise, Alessandra." I lay there thinking about the wedding. *I wonder if Art wants to get married now or wait until the baby is born? Don will be disappointed about the baby. I hope he doesn't lose control.*

When I heard a knock on the door, I looked over. There he was, standing there. *He is so cute. Just as cute as he was when I first met him. I was so in love with him. Now, that's all over. I am in love with someone else.*

"May I come in, Mekia?" Don asked meekly.

"I can call you Mekia, can't I?" he asked.

"Please Don, don't even think about calling me Peaches anymore. She's gone and I'm glad." I looked at him and thought about all the years and time we had wasted, about all the people who had gotten hurt and the sadness I had inside for him.

"The test results came back, Don."

Just as I was going to tell him the results, Art showed up. "Come in, dear. Don, this is Arturo, my fiancé." They looked at each other and nodded their heads. Art gave me the food he brought, and I asked him to wait outside.

Don's temper flared. "How could you mess with a goddamn Italian?"

"Don't you use that tone with me. This is *my* life, not yours."

"Well you know, you are still married to me."

"Don, I've already hired an attorney to file for divorce."

"You did what?"

"You heard me Don. I am filing for a divorce. There is no way I could stay with you."

"What about the baby?" he asked.

"The baby is not yours."

He dropped his head and then looked back up at me. I saw a tear forming in his eye, but he did not let it fall. "I guess there is nothing left for us to say."

"No."

"Everything I did was because I loved you, Mekia. This Italian guy is not who you think he is. I have seen his kind, and they are all slick, smooth operators with ulterior motives." He thought about the name Arturo. He then erased it from his mind. Don left the room and did not look back.

Art came into the room with a smile on his face.

"What are you smiling about?" I asked.

"Well Don left, which means he is not the father of the baby."

"You can stop calling her, *the* baby. It's a girl." He ran over to the bed, picked me up and swung me around. Stop, Arturo, you're making me dizzy."

He stopped and said, "Oh, oh, I am sorry. It's just that I am so excited."

"Her name is Alessandra, after your mother."

"You have made me the happiest man on earth! Wait until I tell the family! I have to get you home and start taking care of you."

I wondered why he did not say anything about the wedding. *Maybe it's a man thing.*

Art arranged for the finest doctors to come to the hospital to check on the baby and me. He wanted to make sure we were okay before we left the hospital. I was impressed with all the things he did in just two days. All reports came back well on me and the baby. Art was pleased. I stayed in the hospital for two more weeks. Art showed up every day with flowers and a box of candy. He even had my food brought into the hospital. He refused to allow us to eat the hospital food. In two weeks, I gained five pounds. Finally, the doctors gave the okay to let me go home. Art was there bright and early to pick me up. He got there around eight.

"Are you ready to go home, my two beautiful girls?"

"Yes, we are!"

I thought about Don and wondered if he was okay. "Did you take the BMW back to Don?"

"Everything has been taken care of. I got all of your things from his house, too." I didn't like the way he said that.

"What is going on Art?"

He stopped helping me pack and said matter-of-factly, "You know, Camilla is still going to have him taken out."

"No, Art, please. You have to do something. Don't let her kill him. He's my son's father!"

He continued packing my bags. "You knew what was going to happen. I told you I would get her to hold off and I did. She held off while you were in the hospital because we did not know what was going to happen with you. I can't ask her to do it again. You don't understand, Peaches..."

I interrupted him. "Please don't call me Peaches anymore. She no longer exists."

"If Camilla lets him live, she'd be telling the world she is weak, and that is one thing she will never do. I am sorry, baby. Let's go."

I've got to warn Don. Maybe he will be able to get away somehow. As we drove home, I tried to figure out how I could tell Don to run.

Chapter 26

Back at Arturo's house.

We finally reached the house; I was exhausted from the drive and fearful this was going to be a long, hard pregnancy. Art took my bags up to the bedroom, and I immediately lay down and fell asleep. When I woke up, Art was not in the room. I got up and went downstairs to see if he was there. The maid was cleaning. "Where is Mr. Arturo?" I asked.

"He has gone out, but he left you a note in the kitchen." I went to the kitchen, anxious to get his note.

It said, "I hope my girls had a wonderful nap. I will be back shortly. I have business to take care of. Love, AB."

I put the note down and immediately ran to the phone to dial Don's number. The phone rang. *"Come on ... answer, answer!"*

He picked up, "Hello?"

"Don, this is Mekia. Listen to me. I mean business. I'm trying to save your life. You must leave town today... now! Camilla has a contract out on you."

"How do you know this?"

"Don't worry about how I know, just trust me and go."

"I can't, Mekia. I can't just leave right now. Besides, how do you know this?"

I paused for a moment. "Because Arturo is her brother. The man I am going to marry. Now you must go." I hung up the phone and prayed that he would take my advice and leave. My heart was heavy, but I felt I had done what I could do to help him. I looked at the phone and erased the outgoing number to Don's house. I did not want Art to know I still had a soft spot in my heart for this man. At least I did it before I married the man. Technically, I wasn't a traitor yet.

Just then, I heard Art parking his car in the garage. I went to the door to greet him. "Hello, baby! I missed you." He looked at me, but did not say anything. "What's the matter?" He acted like he was upset about something.

"Moments ago Camilla called me. She is upset because she got word that Don has left town."

"Did you tip him off, Mekia?" I looked down at the floor, which was a dead giveaway.

"Yes I did, Art. I felt sorry for him."

Art stormed away from me. He went to the bar and made himself a drink. He drank it down in one swallow and then slammed the glass down on the bar. "You cannot interfere with my business, Mekia! That is rule number one in this family. Do you understand?"

In a soft voice, I said, "Yes Art, I understand." I knew I was wrong and I accepted that. He had every reason to be angry with me. As he sat at the bar drinking, I knew I had better not say anything else to him. I left the room and went upstairs, worrying that I had ruined everything. I lay across the bed and started thinking about Katie. I begin to talk to her as if she was there. "Katie, I am almost there. I have found the perfect man. I just hope I have not messed things up by telling Don to run."

Then someone touching me on the shoulder interrupted my thoughts. It was Art. I looked at him as he reached out and hugged me. As we embraced, I told him again how sorry I was for what I had done. "It's okay, Mekia. Just remember you must never interfere with my business. That is a family rule." I nodded in agreement.

As I laid my head on his shoulder, I thought about what Don said to me before he left the hospital. *"Mekia, this Italian guy is not who you think he is. I have seen his kind and they are all slick, smooth operators with ulterior motives."*

I convinced myself that Don was just jealous.

We made up, but I still sensed some tension between us. I looked longingly into Art's eyes, and said, "Make love to me, baby." He looked at me with a strangeness in his eye. However, he said nothing and began to sex me, but not in his usual way. I guess he was thinking about the baby.

When he finished, he sat up on the bed and said, "You are just too good to be true."

I looked at him and smiled. *I love this man. I just hope he feels the same way about me.*

He kissed me and said, "I picked up your divorce papers today from the attorney."

"So it's final. I'm officially divorced."

Then he said, "But I need to talk to you about something else. Come downstairs." He left the room. I took a shower before I went down. When I got downstairs, Art was sitting on the sofa. "Come sit next to me." I sat down next to him and he said, "Do you remember how I told you that I thought Camilla tried to have you killed?"

"Yes."

"Well, I went and asked her if she had anything to do with the accident and she said no. I also told her that you were pregnant and it was a girl."

"What did she say?"

"Well, she has told the entire family that you are pregnant with a girl. Can you believe it? Something finally made this woman happy! She has already started shopping, so don't be surprised if she shows up here with a truckload of things for the baby."

I was happy to hear the good news. Art didn't seen to be mad at me after what I had done by calling Don. I couldn't believe it. I didn't deserve his love or this baby. *When will he make me his wife?* I got up off the sofa and said, "Art, what about the wedding? Do you still plan to marry me now that my divorce from Don is final?"

"Of course I do, baby."

"When?"

"Well, I thought you wanted to wait until after the baby was born before we did that."

"No. I don't want to wait until the baby is born. I want my baby to be born of marriage, not out of wedlock," I started to cry.

He came to me, held my hand and kissed it. "If that is what you want, then that is what we will do. It's not a big deal. I asked you to marry me, remember?" He pointed to the ring on my finger.

"I tell you what. I will make arrangements for us to get married in the judge's chambers for now. Then once the baby is born, we will have a formal ceremony. How does that sound?" I did not plan on marrying him like that, but since I was already pregnant and showing, I agreed. The next day we went downtown to the courthouse and we were married. I became Mrs. Arturo Battista, or Mekia James Battista. I felt wonderful!

Art took me to Hawaii for our honeymoon and we had a ball. We stayed there for a month. I ate so much, I was as big as a house. I did not think much about Don anymore either. I just hoped and prayed that he had made it out okay. I did think about Katie. *If she could just see me now...*

Chapter 27

Back home from Hawaii.
We arrived back from our honeymoon and I was happy to be home. I had a doctor's appointment the next day. Art brought my special bag in the house while the limo driver unpacked the car. I went straight to my bedroom, since I wanted to take a shower to refresh myself. We had a long flight and I was beat. I lay down on the bed and off to sleep I went. I woke up the next morning and Art was up already as usual. I could smell the coffee. I got up, got dressed and

went downstairs. I gave him a good-morning kiss. "You must have been tired. You slept like a brick."

"What does a brick sleep like?"

"I'm just kidding you. Do you want me to drive you to the doctor's office?"

"Well, you don't have to."

"I think I will. I want to." We ate our breakfast and he drove me to the doctor's office.

"Everything went great with the baby," I told him.

"Good! I can't wait until she gets here. I have to stop by the club to check on something. Do you mind going with me, or do you want me to take you home?"

"I want to go to the club. I haven't been there in a long while. You know how much I love that place."

"Yes, I do." We talked about some other things and laughed about stuff we did in the past. I had never been happier in my life.

When we got to the club, Art said, "Stay here until I get back."

"Can't I go in with you?"

He hesitated, then said, "Okay, come on in." He got out of the car and went around to open the door for me. When we got inside the club, I sat at the first table and Art went to the bar to talk to some guys. They seemed to be disagreeing about something, but I couldn't hear what they were saying. Then a young lady came from the back room. I looked at her and she was Italian, a beautiful young lady. She went over to Art and put her arms around his waist.

What is going on here? Art pulled her away from him and said something to her. He pointed at me. She looked at me and left the room.

Art came back over to me and said, "Let's go."

I waited until we got into the car, then I asked, "Who was that young lady in the club?"

"She is someone Camilla sent over to help me run the club."

"She sure wanted to rip your clothes off."

He did not answer. We drove for ten minutes before he said anything. "What do you want to eat?"

"I'm not sure right now. What do you want?"

"I won't be eating at home tonight. I have to go out of town on business."

"Art, honey, I don't want to be by myself tonight."

"Well Mekia, I will have the housekeeper stay over tonight and keep an eye on you, okay?"

I did not respond, because I was upset. He had been in and out of town, so he said, since we returned from our honeymoon. I was beginning to worry. He drove me back to the house, and then he left. I went up to my room, put on my nightclothes and looked for a book to read. I had ordered a book about Italian families and their culture. I started reading and fell asleep.

I was awakened by a noise. Someone was in the house. Then I thought, *Oh the housekeeper is here with me.* I settled back down until I heard the door to the bedroom open.

"Who is there?" It was Camilla and her two bodyguards.

"Camilla, what are you doing here? Why must you visit me like this? It would be nice for you to call on the phone and say, 'Hi, how are you and the baby?' But that would be too easy for you, wouldn't it Camilla?"

She sat down in the chair. "You have a big mouth,

young lady. Lucky for you, you have the Battista princess growing inside of you. She is the only thing keeping you alive. Since you did not take my advice the first time, I am going to give you one last card to play. Once Alessandra is born, leave and go back to your little ghetto life!"

"What do you mean leave? I am married to Arturo now. You can't tell me to leave. Besides, who will take care of my baby?"

She laughed. "The baby belongs to the Battista family. You have three months to decide what you are going to do."

"You can't just kill me and write me off, Camilla. Art won't let you do that."

Camilla laughed her wicked laugh once again. "I really don't want to kill you, Mekia. I just want you out of my family."

"Well, I'm not going to give you my baby, Camilla."

With that, she got up and left the room. I never saw her again.

The next morning, Art came back home. I was so glad to see him. I ran downstairs and kissed him.

"I missed you. Camilla came to see me last night." He looked up at the ceiling.

"Why did she come here? I asked her to stay away from you."

"Camilla wants me to give the baby to her."

"What? She has gone too far now. I must call her. You stay here and listen." He dialed the number and someone answered the phone. "Let me speak to Camilla. Camilla, how could you come here and do that to Mekia last night? You got her all upset. She could have lost the baby or something. I want you to stop your wicked ways and don't come back here to this house ever again!" He hung up the phone. "The nerve of her! She thinks she owns the world. Come here, baby. It will be all right now. She won't be back here to bother you any more."

I was relieved that Art had called Camilla, but I still did not trust that she would stay away from us. Art stayed with me from that day forward. He did not want to chance Camilla coming back and scaring me.

He went with me to all my doctor's appointments and anywhere else I had to go. We were happy with each other, but Camilla had us living in bondage, afraid of her. I could tell Art was afraid of her, too. He tried to be cool about it when we discussed her, but I could see in his eyes that he was not sure what Camilla would do next.

Chapter 28

The baby is coming.

It was around 4:30 in the morning. I had to pee, so I got up and went to the bathroom. It was time for me to have this baby. "Art, Art, come here!"

He ran into the bathroom, still half-asleep. "What is it?"

I smiled. "It is time to have our baby!" He ran to put on his pants, picked me up and carried me to the car. He drove as fast as he could to the hospital. We finally arrived and I was rushed to the delivery room. The baby was already starting to come out. The doctors and nurses were running around as if the President of the United States was in the hospital. The nurse came in and put an IV in my arm. "Where is my husband, Mr. Battista? He should be here with me." She did not say anything. I started to feel drowsy. *What is going on here? I am not supposed to be unconscious!*

"What are you doing to me?" I demanded.

The nurse said, "Please relax and everything will be fine." Those are the last words I remember hearing that day.

When I woke up, I was still in the hospital. I rang for the nurse. When the nurse came into the room, I asked, "When can I see my baby?"

She looked at me. "What baby?"

I sat up in the bed and said, "I just had a baby girl! Where is she?" I starting screaming and yelling, "Where is my baby? Where is my baby?" Another nurse came in and they gave me a shot. The shot made me calm. "Where is my husband?"

The nurse looked at me and said, "I don't know about your husband, Ms. James."

"Why are you calling me, Ms. James? My name is Mrs. Battista!"

The nurse looked at the chart in her hand. "Your chart says you are Mekia James. See?" She showed it to me, and it said Mekia James.

"Why am I here in the hospital then?"

The nurse said, "You were in a car accident three days ago."

I screamed as loudly as I could, "What have you done with my baby?"

The shot they had given me put me to sleep.

The next morning I woke up and the nurse was there in the room. "Wake up! It's time for you to go home, Ms. James." I looked at her and wanted to hit her. I got up and put on my clothes. Here is your purse and the keys to your car. Is there anyone you want to call?" I told her no. She got a wheelchair and pushed me down to the first floor. Then she said, "Take care of yourself." Then she gave me an envelope.

I looked at the keys she gave me and noticed it was a BMW key. I pushed the panic button to see where the car was. The alarm sounded and I found the car. It was the same black 645 BMW that I drove when I was with Johnny, or Don, or whoever. I got into the car and just sat there for a moment. I was still weak and in shock.

I looked at the envelope the nurse gave me. The outside of the envelope said, "OPEN ME." I opened the envelope, and it was a letter from Art.

Dear Mekia,

I know you must be hurting right now, but the pain will go away eventually. Alessandra is a beautiful baby girl. She weighed 7 lb and 10 oz. Her hair is jet black, and her skin is white as a dove. You did a great job carrying her for nine months. No one will ever know her mother is black. I am sorry it had to be this way. My family would have never accepted you, and Camilla would have had you killed, or even worse, she might have killed your son, Mich. Don't worry, Mich is still in school in Paris. I paid for his full tuition. You are probably wondering why I chose you. Let's just say you were a jewel waiting to be

purchased. I left you the house and some money.
There is a total of two million dollars waiting
for you in the safe. Please don't be foolish and
try to find Alessandra or me. Your search will be
fruitless. You will never find us.
    Art

There was a picture of Alessandra in the envelope. I looked at the picture and he was right, she was a beautiful, Italian baby girl.

I never saw Art or my baby again. Trust, but verify.

Afterword

The story you have just read is fictitious; however, switched, stolen, black market babies and baby brokers are real. They have existed for decades, and even today, there remain many black market adoption facilitators and networks in the United States and internationally. They sell switched and stolen babies, as well as voluntarily relinquished babies from unsuspecting parents to unsuspecting adopters. Some adopters, desperate for a child, have knowingly paid huge sums to unscrupulous baby brokers.

These adoptions often become legalized and sealed in the court, not to be discovered until the adult adoptee begins to search for his or her parents. Some of the better known black market baby brokers and large black market operations of the past include: Georgia Tann (Tennessee Children's Home Society), Bessie Bernard (who sold babies in New York and Florida), Hicks Clinic (Alabama), Cole Babies, Hightower, The Veil, and

Crittenton, to name a few. There are many others.

This information was quoted from the Switched, Stolen, Black Market Babies and the Baby Brokers' website. Please visit this site and other websites on this subject for more information.

www.amfor.net - site information provided by: Lori Carangelo

www.geocities.com

www.amfor.net/stolenbabies.html

www.adoptionagencychecklist.com

Good luck in your search. If you need further information on this subject, please e-mail Admin@ thestreet.com

Also available from 5th Street Books

by Elizabeth E. Smith:

Candee

and

In the Shadow of My Sister

5th Street Books
P O Box 391633
Snellville, Georgia 30039
www.5thstreetbooks.com